"Are You In, Or Am I Going It Alone Tomorrow?"

Gina made a split-second decision. She needed this job. "I'm in. Under one condition."

Wade narrowed his eyes. "I don't usually—"

"We keep it strictly business. Agreed?"

Wade's lips thinned, but Gina stood her ground and kept her focus on his unflinching face.

Finally Wade nodded. "I won't do anything you don't want me to do."

Great, she thought ruefully. Wade hadn't agreed to her terms at all.

Dear Reader,

I've always wanted to write a story set on an island. What better place to put Wade and Gina than in a resort I've visited dozens of times during my life, Santa Catalina Island! I'd ride the express boat to make the twenty-two-mile journey from Los Angeles to dock at Avalon Bay, the crescent-shaped harbor that was once a pirate's hideaway.

And to make the story complete, I was fortunate to tap into the expertise of my lifelong friends Allyson and Ross Pearlman, owners of the real catamaran yacht, *Between The Sheets*. I thank them for their sailing tips, the inspiration for the title (I stole it!) and those wonderful times on the water. Thanks to them I had an easy time sending Wade and Gina off on their romantic and rocky adventure!

Sincerely,

Charlene Sands

CHARLENE SANDS

BETWEEN THE CEO'S SHEETS

Silhouette
Desire

Published by Silhouette Books
America's Publisher of Contemporary Romance

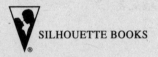

SILHOUETTE BOOKS

ISBN-13: 978-0-373-76805-9
ISBN-10:   0-373-76805-2

BETWEEN THE CEO'S SHEETS

Copyright © 2007 by Charlene Swink

This edition published by arrangement with Harlequin Books S.A.

® and TM are trademarks of Harlequin Books S.A., used under license. Trademarks indicated with ® are registered in the United States Patent and Trademark Office, the Canadian Trade Marks Office and in other countries.

Visit Silhouette Books at www.eHarlequin.com

Printed in U.S.A.

Books by Charlene Sands

Silhouette Desire

The Heart of a Cowboy #1488
Expecting the Cowboy's Baby #1522
Like Lightning #1668
Heiress Beware #1729
Bunking Down with the Boss #1746
Fortune's Vengeful Groom #1783
Between the CEO's Sheets #1805

Harlequin Historical

Lily Gets Her Man #554
Chase Wheeler's Woman #610
The Law and Kate Malone #646
Winning Jenna's Heart #662
The Courting of Widow Shaw #710
Renegade Wife #789
Abducted at the Altar #816

CHARLENE SANDS

resides in Southern California with her husband, high school sweetheart and best friend, Don. Proudly, they boast that their children, Jason and Nikki, have earned their college degrees. The empty nesters now have two cats that have taken over the house. Charlene's love of the American West, both present and past, stems from storytelling days with her imaginative father, which sparked a passion for a good story and her desire to write romance. When not writing, she enjoys sunny California days, Pacific beaches, and sitting down with a good book.

Charlene invites you to visit her Web site at www.charlenesands.com to enter her contests, stop by for a chat, read her blog and see what's new! E-mail her at charlenesands@hotmail.com.

To my husband, Don, sole owner of my heart.
And to Jason and Nikki our wonderful children
who always make us proud.

One

It was the last place Gina Grady wanted to be.

But desperation was an unwelcome persuasion. And Gina was just that: desperate. Her pride and determination also played in the mix.

She needed this job.

She needed to stay in L.A.

Gina was ushered into an empty office. "Mr. Beaumont will be right with you," Mrs. Danner from Human Resources announced before exiting the office, leaving Gina alone with her thoughts.

She walked over to the massive floor-to-ceiling window and took in the view from the twelfth floor of the trendy Santa Monica high-rise, praying the interview would go well. She shouldn't be so worried.

Sam Beaumont had been her friend once. He'd always been kind. Yet, having to take him up on his offer of a job at the Triple B ranked with her top-ten most desperate acts of survival. The Beaumont name alone caused her insides to quake and she wondered at her own sanity in coming. However, it wasn't Sam but his younger brother, Wade, she hoped never to cross paths with again.

The Pacific Ocean loomed on the horizon, the pounding blue surf and white caps filling the view. She shuddered at the sight, and shook off her thoughts of Wade. She had enough to worry about without letting old fears get the better of her today.

She owed money to a whole lot of people and they didn't give a damn that she'd been swindled by a con man she had once trusted as her partner. GiGi Designs, the company she'd struggled to conceive hadn't been given a chance. Her lifelong dream had been destroyed in the blink of an eye. All that she'd worked so hard for had come crumbling down around her.

Now Gina was even more determined to rebuild her clothing design business—from the ground up, if need be.

But first, she needed to pay off her debts.

Gina tidied her long dark hair, making sure it hadn't fallen from the tight knot at the back of her head, straightened her black pinstriped suit and took a seat in front of the massive oak desk, setting her black knockoff Gucci handbag on her lap. She waited for Sam to enter his office.

She closed her eyes to steady her wayward nerves. Calmer, she took a deep breath before opening them again. But when she glanced down, she simply stared in disbelief at the nameplate outlined in solid brass on the desk:

Wade Beaumont, CEO.

"No!" Her heart thudding against her chest, she rose abruptly. She couldn't bear to see Wade again, much less work for him. She couldn't possibly swallow that much pride. She set her purse strap on her shoulder and turned to leave.

"Running away again, Gina?"

Stunned, Gina stopped abruptly and stared into the dark-green eyes of Wade Beaumont. His head cocked to one side, he was leaning against the door where she'd hoped to make her escape. He stared back at her, his lips curled into a mocking smile. "You do that so well."

Gina kept her head held high and tried to appear calm while her insides quivered uncontrollably. She'd foolishly hoped that Wade had nothing to do with Triple B, but now she'd seen the folly in that.

But she couldn't deny how handsome Wade was, standing there in a pair of black trousers and a crisp white shirt, the sleeves rolled up to his elbows. He looked older, more mature and those bold green eyes—she'd never forget the way they use to soften when he looked at her. Or the way his strong body felt crushed up against hers.

Or the day, nine years ago, when she'd run away from him.

"I…this is a mistake. I shouldn't have come," she said on a breath.

Wade ignored her comment. "You applied for a job."

"Yes, I, um assumed Sam would be running your father's company."

"Ah, so you didn't think you'd find me here?"

Gina bolstered her courage as she recalled Wade's onetime contempt for the company his father seemed to love more than his own two sons. Triple B was all Blake Beaumont had ever cared about. When she'd known him back in El Paso, she'd understood Wade's retreat from both the company and his father. She'd never have guessed that he would be at the helm now. Never. "No, I didn't actually. As I said, this is a mistake."

Gina watched his mouth twitch. He walked around his desk and picked up her resume, reading it over carefully.

"I run Triple B now from the West Coast. My father's dead and my brother's remarried and living in Texas. The company fell into my hands some time ago." He stared directly into her eyes. "I suppose you thought I'd work all my life on Uncle Lee's ranch or wind up with a small place of my own back in El Paso?"

"Actually, I hadn't given it much thought," Gina said truthfully. She had thought of Wade countless times in the past—dreamed of him and wondered how his life had turned out—but she never cared what he did for a living. It had never mattered to her.

She'd met Wade while living with the Buckleys in El Paso for the summer. Sarah, her college roommate, had been there for her after her parents had died in a boating accident. Gina had been on the boat, narrowly escaping death that day. Sarah had seen to the funeral, making all the arrangements. She'd held Gina tight, when the caskets were lowered into the ground. And after, when Gina had been uncertain of her future, Sarah had taken her home to El Paso.

The Buckleys' place neighbored Wade's uncle's ranch and the four of them—Sam, Wade, Sarah and Gina—had been inseparable. She came to depend on their friendship and slowly began to heal from her terrible loss, until the day when her world had come crashing down upon her once again.

And now, Wade sat down at his desk and leaned back studying her, his eyes raking her over. She felt exposed and vulnerable, yet unable to draw herself away from his intense scrutiny.

"You hadn't thought about me? Of course, why would you? My father took care of that, didn't he?" He gestured for her to sit down, not expecting an answer. "Take a seat. We'll do this interview."

"No, I—I don't think that would be a good idea, Wade."

"I thought you needed a job?" he said, narrowing his eyes on her.

"I do need a job." She directed her gaze to his without apology. "Just not this one."

He looked down at her resume. "You're more than qualified."

Gina's legs wobbled, so she decided to take a seat, at least for the moment.

"You've got a degree in business. And then you went on to the Fashion Institute. Did my father's money finance that?"

He asked that question so casually that Gina had to rewind his words in her mind to make sure she'd heard him correctly. Wade believed that she'd taken his father's bribe—dirty money that she'd never wanted—to stay away from him.

He believed it because she'd never denied it. She'd let him think that she'd been enticed by a large sum of money to leave El Paso.

But that hadn't been the case at all.

She'd run out on Wade for an entirely different reason. And to have Wade believe she'd accepted his father's bribery had guaranteed that he wouldn't come after her.

She'd hated what he'd done to her.

Hated the high and mighty Blake Beaumont even more.

But if given the choice all over again, Gina wouldn't have changed anything about that summer. Except the night that they made love. Though the sweet memories of the intense passion they shared were always with her, she wished she could take that night back.

Slinging her purse on her shoulder and holding her anger in check, she stood to leave. "I'm sorry," she said, and his dark brows lifted, lining his forehead. "For wasting your time."

Wade stood and glared at her. "You didn't. You're hired."

* * *

Wade watched Gina blink her gorgeous espresso eyes. Nine years had only added to her sultry beauty and it angered him that she could still make his heart race. All Wade had to do was look into those dark, deceitful eyes and admire that voluptuous body and he had trouble remembering the pain she'd caused him. He'd taken her virginity and it had been the highest of highs, claiming her as his own.

She'd run out on him then, leaving town, without so much as a goodbye. She'd gotten what she'd wanted—a load of money from his manipulative father. But if money had been her goal she should have waited. No longer the poor young man working on his uncle's ranch, Wade was floating in cash. But she'd been bought off long ago and had caused Wade enough steaming heartache to fill a Mississippi riverboat.

Gina straightened her pinstriped suit, her chest heaving, the structured material unable to hide the fullness of her breasts. Wade looked his fill, watching the rise and fall as she tried to hide her hot Irish-Italian temper.

Rosy-lipped, with a full flush of color on her light-olive skin, Gina was still the most beautiful woman he had ever seen. From the moment she'd shown up in Aunt Dottie's kitchen with an offering of fresh Italian bread and homemade pasta sauce, Wade had been a goner. She'd knocked him to his knees.

"No. But thank you."

She spoke the words carefully and instincts told Wade that she'd been tempted to take the job. Hell, one look at her and he knew he couldn't let her walk out of his office. Not until they finished what they'd started nine years ago.

"There's a big bonus involved," he said, catching her attention. Her brows lifted provocatively. He shrugged. "I'm in a bind. My personal assistant chose last month to get pregnant. She's down with acute morning sickness and took disability leave. The other qualified assistants are busy with their own projects."

"How big a bonus?" she asked. Wade knew he'd gotten her attention once again. Money, it seemed, spoke volumes with her. Why was he disappointed? He'd known the sort of woman she was, but he had to admit that back in his youth, she sure had him fooled. "It's a thousand dollars a week to start and once the project is settled, win or lose, you get a ten-thousand-dollar bonus. But I'll warn you, you'll be working long hours. Take it or leave it, Gina."

He could almost see her mind working, calculating, *figuring*. She must need a job badly. Wade had the upper hand and he knew it. She was tempted.

He sat down at his desk and rifled through papers, coming up with information on the Catalina project. He had figures to check and hours of work to do before making a bid on the biggest contract Triple B might hope to gain.

He felt her presence, breathed in the heady scent

of her exotic perfume. His better judgment told him to let her go. He'd be better off not complicating his life by choosing to work alongside the only woman he knew who could turn him on with just one look. He'd had to sit down to conceal an unwelcome yet healthy erection that pulsed from underneath the desk.

He must be crazy.

"I must be crazy, but I accept," she said softly.

Wade lifted his head and nodded, more satisfied than he wanted to be. "I expect a decent hard day's work from my employees. If you can manage that, you've got the job."

Her chin jutted up. "I can manage that. I always give one hundred percent."

Wade's mind drifted back to his uncle's barn that night so many years ago. She'd given one hundred percent of herself to him, generously offering up her body with passion and pleasure, but it had all been a trap.

This time, he'd have to be more careful.

"I'll pick you up later this afternoon. Oh, and dress comfortably. We'll be working at my home through the evening."

Gina recalled Wade's instructions and wondered at her sanity. She would never have taken this job if the compensation hadn't been so tempting. She had debtors knocking on her door and that big bonus Wade had offered would surely keep them happy for a while.

She'd changed her clothes three times before settling on a pair of white slacks and a soft-pink knit top. She brought the whole outfit together with a matching short sweater. Comfortable, but still a professional enough look for a woman about to embark on a new job with an old lover.

Gina shook her head. She still had trouble believing she would be working with Wade Beaumont after all these years. He resented her. She'd seen it in his eyes each time he glanced at her. No amount of Beaumont charm could conceal that look.

Gina lifted her briefcase filled with documents that Wade had asked her to review this afternoon. She glanced around the tiny guest apartment she lived in behind the large Spanish-style house in the Hollywood Hills. Once Wade saw where and how she lived, he would realize how desperate she'd been for this job. It was a tidy place with three rooms: a small cozy living space with one sofa, a kitchen that amounted to one wall of the living room with a range, a refrigerator and a café table for two, and a bedroom beyond that.

Her apartment suited her needs. She'd had to downsize everything in her life since Mike Bailey had betrayed her. They'd dreamed the same dreams, or so she had thought, and had gone into partnership together. The day GiGi Designs was born was the happiest day in Gina's life. The day she found out he'd absconded with all of her money and designs only compared with the day she'd had to leave El Paso and Wade Beaumont forever. She'd been heartbroken on both accounts.

Gina sighed and walked out the door, deciding to meet Wade out front. Not a minute later, he drove up in a shining black Lexus convertible. She watched him get out and approach her, his eyes focused on her clothes and she wondered if he approved of her choice of attire. Though not one of her original designs, she always chose her outfits carefully. When the door of the main house slammed, Gina turned her head to find the owner locking up.

"Hey there, Gina. Are you going out?" Marcus's eyes narrowed on Wade and she couldn't help but laugh. Her handsome fifty-something landlord was always watching out for her.

"Yes, but it's business. I have a new job."

"Ah. Well then, good luck." He headed for his car in the driveway.

"Ciao, Marcus. See you tomorrow."

When Gina turned back around, Wade's intense-green eyes burned into hers. "Do you live with him?"

Gina blinked away her anger. Wade had no right to ask her personal questions. She wondered why it mattered, anyway. He had nothing but contempt for her. "No. I don't live with him. I live in the guesthouse in the back."

Wade's mouth twitched. "How convenient." He put his hand to her lower back and ushered her inside his car. She took her seat and adjusted the seatbelt as Wade started the ignition. He took one last look at the house and gunned the engine. They drove in silence for a while, until he asked, "Is that guy married?"

Gina leaned her head back against the seat and smiled inwardly. Marcus and Delia had the kind of marriage her parent's had had. That kind of love and commitment was rare and it saddened Gina to think that her parents' love had been cut short by a freakish accident. "Yes, happily."

"He's your landlord?"

"My landlord and a very dear friend."

Wade shot her another glance, this time with a dubious look in his eyes. Gina let the subject drop and stared out the window, her eyes focused on the mountain on one side of the road rather than the blue ocean waters on the other. As Wade drove down Pacific Coast Highway, the wind blew her long hair out of its tight knot.

Ten minutes later and completely wind-blown, Gina was pinning her hair back up, noting Wade's eyes on her as he killed the engine. She marveled at the impressive two-story house that sat on a strip of beach in the Malibu Colony. Wade hopped out of the car and came around to open her door. She stood and looked around for a moment, her gaze traveling past the house to the surging surf and then beyond to the stunning western horizon. "All of this is yours?"

Wade grabbed her briefcase from the car then nodded, staring directly into her eyes. "It's mine." She shivered from the cold assessing look he cast her; a look that said, "It could have been yours, too."

Or maybe Gina had imagined that. It had been nine long years and surely Wade hadn't brooded over her too long. Handsome and successful, Wade wouldn't have to look far for female companion-ship. He had all the markings of a man used to getting his way with women and with life in general.

Gina followed Wade through the front door and into a large vestibule. From there it seemed that she could almost touch the pounding surf as the shore came into view with brilliant clarity through enormous windows. "Take a look around," he said without ceremony. "I'm going up to take a quick shower."

Gina watched him toss both of their briefcases down onto a soft moss-green L-shaped sofa before disappearing up a winding staircase. She felt safest standing there waiting in the safety of the living room, but curiosity forced her to walk through the French doors that led onto a sweeping veranda over-looking the ocean. Wade seemed to have all things necessary for the life of a single man; a hot tub sur-rounded by a cocktail bar sat in one corner of the deck while a fire pit took up the other corner. In the middle of the deck, patio tables and chairs were arranged to enjoy the view of waves crashing into the sand.

Gina walked to the wooden railing and closed her eyes. Taking a deep breath she tried to calm her jittery nerves, but the combination of deep waters and Wade was too much for her.

Wade approached with two glasses of white wine. He handed her one. "To unwind."

Gina accepted the glass, grateful for the forti-tude, and both of them stood leaning on the railing, gazing out. "It looks peaceful here."

Wade sipped his wine. "Looks can be deceiving."

That's exactly what Gina thought, but she was thinking of the deceptive calm of the uncompromising sea. She was certain Wade meant something altogether different.

Rather than stare at the ocean, she shifted slightly so that she could consider Wade Beaumont. His dark hair, still damp from the shower, was slicked back and tiny drops of water glistened on his neck. Late afternoon sunlight revealed a gleam in his eyes and highlighted high cheekbones leading to a beautiful mouth and the masculine line of his jaw. He had changed into a pair of tight-fitting jeans and a black polo shirt. Tan and trim with broad shoulders, his shirt couldn't hide the strength of his powerfully built chest.

Now, as in the past, Gina had trouble keeping her eyes off of Wade. He affected her like no other man ever had. Her heart pumped twice as hard when he looked at her and an unwelcome tremble stirred her body when he came near. In those clothes, he reminded her of the man she'd once known during a time in her life when she could enjoy carefree days and hot summer nights.

Gina took small sips of her wine. She wasn't much of a drinker and needed to remain in control. She couldn't afford any more slipups.

"Only one more sip," she said, "or my head won't be clear for business." Gina set the glass down on the table. Turning to Wade, she hoped that he would take the hint and lead her back inside so that they could begin their work together. She needed to prove herself on this job and, more importantly, she needed to keep her mind on business and not the glowing attributes of her new boss.

Wade didn't move from his stance by the railing. He shook his head, his eyes fixed on hers. "Sorry, Gina," he said, looking anything but sorry. "I can't work with you."

I can't work with you.

Gina blinked as Wade's words sunk in. A rapid shot of dread coursed through her system. She'd begun to think of this job as a means to an end. And she'd resigned herself to working with Wade, whether she liked it or not. Now, just like that, he dropped a bomb on her plans. What kind of game was he playing? She couldn't control the anger in her voice, "I thought you hired me today?"

Wade slammed his glass down on the top rail and turned the full force of his words on her. "Yes, I hired you. Did you think I'd let you walk out of my office without an explanation? Did you think I'd let you go again? You ran away from me nine years ago and I need to know why."

Two

Shocked, Gina stared into Wade's stormy eyes. When she finally spoke, it was softly and devoid of emotion. "We were young."

She had died that night. Leaving Wade had destroyed her and it had been a long hard road getting her life back. She didn't want to dwell on the past or how her friend Sarah had duped her into leaving Wade. The truth had come out a few years later, and she'd long since forgiven Sarah. But the fact remained: Gina had left Wade in El Paso after one secret, glorious night with him.

"Not that young, Gina. You'd graduated from college. We weren't exactly kids."

"My parents died that year. I didn't know what to do or how…or how I would survive."

"My father solved that problem for you, didn't he? He paid you off. And you took the money and ran, for all you were worth."

Yes, Gina had taken Blake Beaumont's money. It had given her a way out of a very serious dilemma. She'd fallen in love with Wade and the night she'd given him her virginity had been wonderful. She'd hoped for a future with Wade, but thinking back on it now, she wondered if she'd been too clouded by grief to see the truth. Later that night all of her hopes had come crashing down around her.

Sarah was pregnant and she'd named Wade as the father.

Gina went to bed that night, tears falling uncontrollably and her heart aching at how she'd been betrayed by the one man who had given her a measure of comfort and happiness after the death of her parents.

Blake Beaumont's offer had come at exactly the right moment. She'd wanted to hurt Wade for his calculated cruelty. She'd wanted to make him pay for his betrayal. She'd hated him.

She remembered so vividly standing there, face to face with the older man who had abandoned his two sons in favor of building his company. Triple B had been Blake's passion, not the two sweet young boys he'd pawned off on his sister and her husband to raise.

Blake Beaumont slid an envelope her way. "Take the money and this airline ticket and leave El Paso. You're a distraction Wade can't afford right now. I sacrificed his childhood so that he would one day stand beside me and run the company and that time has almost come. Sam, Wade and I, we'll build an enormous empire together. There's no room in it for you, dear."

Gina's first instinct was to rip the check up and toss it into Blake Beaumont's smug face. The selfish man wanted his son's full attention. He wanted to dictate his life—a life that didn't include love. Blake Beaumont had made it clear that he fully intended for Wade to immerse himself in Triple B. The only relationship he wanted for Wade was one of dedicated service to the company.

If her heart hadn't been broken, Gina would have laughed at the irony. Blake wanted her out of the picture but how would he feel knowing that it was really Sarah and her unborn child that would disrupt his plans? Gina had wished she could have stayed around long enough to see the look on Blake Beaumont's face when he realized his troubles were just beginning.

Gina accepted the check and ticket out of town. She knew Blake was too ruthless not to tell Wade about the bribe. And that's what she'd counted on.

Wade had a baby on the way with Sarah and that had been all that mattered. Sarah hadn't known about Gina's feelings for Wade and she'd kept it that way. By accepting his father's bribe, Gina guaranteed that Wade would stay in El Paso with his family. She'd hoped that he would realize his responsibilities to Sarah, too.

Gina lost contact with Sarah then, deciding to deal with her pain in her own way. She moved to Los Angeles and dug her heels in, determined to make a good life for herself. It wasn't until a few years later that Sarah had come looking for Gina with the whole truth.

"Answer me, Gina. Why did you run away?"

"I had good reason, Wade. It's not important now. But you have to believe that leaving El Paso when I did broke my heart."

"It broke your heart?" he said, coming to stand right in front of her, his anger almost tangible. "Funny, but I remember it differently. I remember you letting me strip you naked and take you in my uncle's barn. I remember every little moan, every whimper, every time you cried out my name. I never once heard you say your heart was broken and that you were leaving town the next day."

Tears welled in Gina's eyes and her body trembled with unspoken grief. She had loved Wade then and had felt the cold slap of his betrayal. She shed tears all the way to Los Angeles, but had made up her mind not to look back.

"Wade, when I came to see you that night I didn't know I would be leaving so soon. I…wanted you."

Wade let out a derisive laugh. "And Gina always gets what she wants, right?"

Gina hadn't gotten what she wanted. She'd lost her best friend that summer and the man she'd loved.

Wade had been so sweet, so caring. Once he kissed her and touched her skin, she'd reacted with primal, desperate need. She'd wanted Wade, thought maybe they could have a future together. His every touch and caress excited her, warmed her, told her that she'd been smart to wait to give up her virginity to the right man. They'd spoken of love and the future in vague terms, the relationship too new to know for sure. But Gina fully believed that Wade Beaumont had been the right man for her.

"It wasn't like that," she said in a calm voice, one that she almost didn't recognize.

But Wade didn't really want her explanation. He wanted to lash out. "You were a virgin, Gina. Don't think that didn't weigh on me. I wasn't a boy. I was a twenty-one-year-old man. I didn't know if I'd hurt you physically or emotionally. I didn't know what to think. I was half out of my mind when I learned that you had left El Paso the next day, catching the soonest flight out of town.

"I made the mistake of telling dear old Dad that I'd found the right girl for me during a phone conversation days earlier. Even before we made love, I knew I wanted you in my life. Next thing I know my father makes a rare visit to El Paso. He couldn't wait to tell me that you'd taken a hefty bribe from him. The man was so damn cocky. He didn't realize that I'd hate him for his part in it. He thought I'd appreciate knowing that I'd been wrong about you. But it didn't matter anymore. I pretty much wrote you off as the biggest mistake of my life."

His harsh words cut like a knife. He didn't know the agony she had gone through that night, her emotions running hot and cold, thrilled to have finally given herself to him only to find out later that he had been deceitful. She managed to bolster her courage and hoist her chin. "If that's the case, why did you bother seeing me today? Why did you *hire* me?"

"Because Sam asked me to. I did it as a favor to him, Gina. And now we're stuck with each other."

She gasped silently from the immediate shock to her system. She'd seen Sam a few months ago, crossing paths with him at the airport, his new family in tow. They'd exchanged pleasantries and when he'd found out that she was living in Los Angeles he'd offered her a job if she ever needed one.

With her pride deeply injured, Gina shot back. "Consider yourself, unstuck. I won't ask you to work with the *biggest mistake of your life.*"

Gina turned her back on Wade and walked toward the French doors. She wanted out, away from Wade for good. But just as she stepped inside the house, Wade grabbed her from behind, his hands holding her gently just under her breasts, the zipper of his jeans grinding into her derriere. She felt the pins being pulled from her hair, freeing the tresses from their knotted prison. Wade wove his hand in her hair and brought his lips to her throat, his voice a gruff whisper. "Don't run away again."

Gina's traitorous body reacted to Wade and, angry as she was, she couldn't deny the overwhelming heat pulsing through her. "You don't want me here."

"That may be true." And then he added softly, "But I need you."

Gina slammed her eyes shut. She felt herself softening to Wade and when she turned in his arms to face him, she witnessed the depth of his sincerity. "You need me?"

She glanced at his mouth just as his lips came down onto hers. He cupped her face and deepened the kiss, slanting his mouth over hers again and again. Gina reacted with a little whimper, urging her body closer. His heat was a fire that burned her. And when she sighed, he took the opportunity to drive his tongue into her mouth, mating them together. Soon, Gina's body swayed in rhythm and Wade wrapped his hands around her waist, his fingers pressing into the curve of her buttocks, drawing her closer.

She felt his erection, the hot pulsing need rubbing into her. Heart pounding out of control, she felt dizzy and wanted Wade with undeniable urgency.

"Yoo-hoo, Wa-ade? Are you home? I brought you chili, honey. Just the way you like it, hot and spicy," the low throaty rasp of a woman's voice startled Gina. She pulled away from Wade in time to see a young redhead coming up the deck steps from the beach. In a flowery bikini covered only by a hip-riding sarong, the woman held a hot bowl in her pot-holder-clad hands. She stopped up short when she reached the deck, finding Wade and Gina together. "Oh, sorry, Wade. I guess I had the wrong night. I thought we were on for the hot tub. My mistake," she said casually. "I'll just leave this here for you." She set the chili on the deck table.

"Shoot, Veronica. Sorry. I forgot." He winked at her and smiled. "I'm working tonight."

"I can see that," she said, taking a quick glance at Gina, before backing down the stairs. "Don't work too hard, honey." Gina heard her chuckle as she disappeared onto the beach.

Gina stared at Wade and abruptly everything became clear. For a moment she thought that she was back in El Paso with the young, sweet man she had given herself to unconditionally. Suddenly, she felt foolish. And stupid for thinking that nothing had changed, when, actually, everything had.

She tried to brush past him to get away, but he was like a block of granite, too strong to move without his willing surrender. He reached for her arms and held her without budging. When she glared into his eyes, he shrugged and said calmly, "She's a friend."

Gina wasn't a fool. She doubted Wade had female "friends" who came over just for a quick meal and a splash in the hot tub. She shook her head adamantly. "I think not. I'd better go. Will you drive me home or shall I take a taxi?"

"Neither. We have work to do. When I said I needed you, I meant it. I need a personal assistant for this project and we have to catch you up on the details."

"You mean you'd give up your hot-tub date?" Her voice was deliberately rich with sarcasm.

"I just did, didn't I?" Wade shot back.

Gina bristled. "Yes, you did. You dismissed her quite easily. But what about what just happened between us? Can you dismiss *that* just as easily?" His kiss had stole Gina's breath, but she had regained normal breathing.

Wade pursed his lips. He stared at hers, well-ripened and swollen from his powerful assault. "I never could dismiss you, Gina. You're hardly the kind of woman a man can forget."

"That does not answer my question."

"Listen, maybe I was out of line a minute ago. But I'm not kidding when I say I need you. As my assistant. We're setting sail first thing tomorrow so—"

Gina snapped her head up. "Setting sail? For where?"

"For Catalina island. You should have been briefed during the first interview with Helen in Personnel. It was a stipulation of the job."

Wade seemed full of surprises. First he stunned her with that incredible kiss and now this unexpected announcement of an island trip. "I wasn't informed about a trip."

"You knew about the latest project the company plans to bid on. It could be the biggest contract in Triple B's history and I intend to get it. It's right there in the file I gave you to review."

"Yes, but I didn't think—"

"It's the reason for the big bonus, Gina," he interrupted to clarify.

"But that's what I don't understand. That's a great

deal of money for a trip to Catalina. It's only a few hours away. Surely, one day isn't worth such a large sum of money."

"One day? Gina, we'll be on that island for a minimum of one week and I guarantee you'll be working long hours."

Gina slumped her shoulders. "One week?"

He nodded. "Seven days, including the weekend. So are you in or am I going it alone tomorrow?"

Gina slammed her eyes shut. She hated her own cowardice. She hadn't been on the water in any capacity since the boat accident that claimed her parents' lives. She'd dealt with the guilt at being the sole survivor, but she hadn't been forced to face her fear—until now. And she was ready. She'd been praying to find a way to conquer her anxiety and now she had the opportunity. If she didn't face her fears, she'd not only lose the revenue to rebuild her future, she'd lose part of herself all over again.

Gina made a split-second decision. She needed this job for more than one reason. But she would accept the position under one condition, and one condition only. "I'm in. Under one condition."

Wade narrowed his eyes. "I don't usually—"

"We keep it strictly business." Gina had allowed personal feelings to get the better of her in business once before and that had landed her with a pile of bills, slimy pawnshop receipts and creditors pounding on her door. She couldn't let that happen again to her pocketbook or her heart. "Agreed?"

Wade's lips thinned.

She stood her ground and kept her focus on his unflinching face.

Finally Wade nodded. "I won't do anything you don't want me to do. Now, let's go over those files. I don't want to get you home late. We'll be setting sail at eight sharp."

Gina drew in a deep breath wondering how she would fare spending her days and *nights* with the only man who could anger her, confuse her and make her ache desperately for his touch.

I won't do anything you don't want me to do.

Great, she thought ruefully. She'd just realized that Wade hadn't agreed to her terms at all, but instead, issued her a challenge.

She felt herself slowly sinking and she had to paddle fast to keep from going under. Which was saying something for a woman who had a dire fear of water.

Three

The next morning, Wade watched Gina make her way down the ramp that led to his docking slip at Marina del Rey. He'd told her to dress comfortably for the trip over to the island but as he watched her descend the steps he was almost sorry he'd given her that instruction. Her flowery sundress hugged her body perfectly and the tight white jacket she wore only accentuated her full breasts and slender waistline. July breezes lifted the hem enough to show her shapely legs as she strolled toward him. She'd pinned her hair in that knot again, but the breezy weather wouldn't allow it and those chestnut tresses fanned out in tempting disarray. The vision she created of simple elegance and unquestionable beauty turned heads at the marina. Wade winced as he caught men stop what they were doing on their boats to watch her walk by.

Wade muttered a curse and told himself this was a business trip where he needed to keep his focus. He'd never let a woman get in the way of what was important to the company. Yet, when Gina approached his yacht he had a hard time remembering that. He peered up from the stern of the boat to greet her. "Morning," he said, none too pleasantly.

"Good morning," she said, but her eyes weren't on him, or his yacht. They focused off in the distance, to the ocean that lay beyond the calm marina.

"You're right on time."

She took her eyes off the ocean long enough to answer, "Thanks to the driver you sent to pick me up." She bit down on her lip and stood there looking quite businesslike, her chin at an unapproachable tilt and her stance slightly rigid. But that dress…that dress could make a man forget his own name.

"Come aboard," he said, putting a hand out to help her.

She scanned the length of the boat and drew a deep breath as if steadying her nerves.

"You haven't changed your mind, have you?" he asked.

She gazed once more at the ocean beyond the marina and shook her head, but her soft tentative answer left room for doubt. "No."

Wade gestured with his outstretched hand. "Come on, Gina. We have to set sail soon."

From the minute he'd seen it, Wade had known he had to own this fifty-two-foot Jeanneau sloop. It hadn't mattered that he didn't know how to sail. He'd made it a hobby and a far-reaching goal to master the craft when he'd first arrived in California. And he'd never been sorry.

Gina's gaze scanned the deck and the steps leading to the quarters below. "I don't see the crew? Are they late?"

"You're looking at the crew."

Gina's dark almond-shaped eyes opened wide. "You?"

"Sam's the pilot in the family and I'm the sailor." He stepped from the boat onto the ramp and grabbed the suitcase from her hand. "Come aboard and I'll show you around."

After a moment's hesitation, Gina accepted his help and he guided her down onto his boat, releasing her the moment her feet hit the deck.

"I had no idea this was how we would arrive in Catalina."

Wade had purposely left that detail out. He didn't know how she would've reacted to his sailing them across to the island. Some people got jittery when they realized only one man had full charge of the boat. But that was what appealed to him most about sailing—the solitude and the challenge of being at the helm. And since he'd had a hard enough time convincing Gina to take the job last night, he'd thought it best to leave their travel arrangements out of the conversation.

His old man once told him that timing was every-thing. Wade believed him. He knew that after that kiss last night and then the untimely appearance from Veronica, he was on shaky enough ground with Gina. She'd been ready to walk out of his life again.

But that kiss had him tied up in knots all night long. Gina had melted in his arms. That much hadn't changed. She'd tasted like wine, her lips soft and full and ripe. Her body molded to his, they fit each other like two puzzle pieces. He couldn't hide his reaction to her any more than she could to him. Wade had lost himself in that kiss and he realized that he couldn't let her go until they'd cleared up all of their unfin-ished business. Then and only then, would he say farewell to Gina for good.

"Can't say that I ever imagined I'd get you on Total Command."

Gina arched her brow. "Excuse me?"

"*Total Command.* The name of the boat. And the only way I operate these days.

Gina cast him a disapproving look.

"Listen, I'll get us both to the island safe and sound. There's no need to worry." Wade picked up her travel bag and stepped down into the living quarters of the boat first and reached for her hand. She advanced carefully down the steps. But when the boat rocked slightly, she lurched forward. Wade grabbed her and their eyes met as their bodies collided. Intense heat sizzled between them. She was soft where she needed to be soft, and firm in all the right places. Wade held her for only a second before stepping aside.

He showed her the open space that would serve as a living room and then they walked through the galley where he had fixed them a mid-morning snack of fresh fruit, cheese and coffee.

Next he explained about the VHF radio and the SSB, the Single Sideband system used for a wider perimeter of communication. He'd even explained to her how she should call for help in case of an emergency. "But don't worry about that. The weather is clear, the wind perfect, I'm in good health and we'll be in Catalina before lunchtime."

Gina nodded, but he didn't miss her wide-eyed expression when he described to her how she could reach the coast guard if necessary.

"And what's in there?" she asked gesturing toward a doorway.

"The master bedroom and bath. There's two more bedrooms on the opposite end of the boat."

"You don't expect, uh, you don't expect me to sleep down here."

Wade wouldn't get a lick of work done if she did. "That's not in your job description. You'll have a room in the finest inn on the island."

"And you?" she asked. "Where will you be?"

"Right here. I stay on the boat when we moor. I don't get as much time as I'd like on the boat. So I've set up an office in one of the spare bedrooms."

He guided her back to the stairs, catching a whiff of her perfume, some exotic fragrance that reminded him of sultry tropical nights. As she climbed up the steps to the top deck he admired the wiggle of her bottom and those long tanned legs as he followed her up.

"Ready?" he asked.

She drew another deep breath into her lungs then put on dark sunglasses. She looked mysterious in them, a superstar trying to conceal her identity. And in a way Gina was a mystery to him. He didn't know her mind, how it worked, what made her tick. He'd known her body and, hopefully, would try his best to know it again, but he would never believe he knew what she was thinking. He refused to make that mistake again.

Wade prepared the yacht for their departure, untying the ropes and setting the sails. Soon they were moving through the marina, past the rocks that harbored the bay, picking up wind that would take them into the Pacific Ocean.

Gina shook with fear the moment the boat began its journey out of the calm marina waters. She took a seat in the cockpit area as salty sea spray lightly drizzled her. With slight desperation she tried to block out images of the last time she'd been on the water, the last time she'd seen her parents alive.

She prayed for enough courage to sustain her through this trip and placed her faith in Wade and his sailing abilities. She watched him move along the sheets and sails, making adjustments and setting the course.

In faded blue jeans and a white tank, Wade might have looked like a typical sailor except his muscles strained harder, his body held more steadfastly, the concentration on his face appeared deeper than on any man she had ever known. Studying his fluid movements along the rigging, Gina could only admire him.

His kiss last night had been *something*.

But it had meant nothing to him.

I need you.

Yes, she understood that he needed her as his personal assistant, a right-hand man and a secretary all rolled up in one. He didn't need her in any other capacity. Not in the way she had needed him nine years ago.

Wade took his place behind the wheel and they sailed in silence for a short time. The boat rocked and waves smashed up against the hull as they sailed along. Gina shuddered, unable to suppress the trembling of her body.

Wade turned at that very instant, catching her in a moment of fear. Their eyes held for a moment before he angled around again and Gina hugged her middle, tamping down the tremors that passed through her.

A few minutes later, Wade left the wheel and handed her a life jacket. "Put this on. You'll feel better."

Gina didn't bother to protest. He was right. But though wearing a life vest might help with her fear, it wouldn't erase the memories she had locked away that were surfacing. She put her arms through the armholes and closed the jacket taut.

Wade helped her fasten the snaps and tied it for her. And when she thought he would return to the wheel, he surprised her by taking a seat by her side. "Feeling seasick?"

She shook her head. Her queasiness had nothing to do with the motion of the sea. "No."

"You're trembling and pale, Gina."

"I'm not—"

"You are."

"No, I meant to say, I'm not seasick, but this is the first time I've been on the water since…the accident."

Wade's dark brows rose. He appeared genuinely surprised.

"I realize that this is the ocean and the accident happened on a lake, but—"

"You haven't been on the water since?" he asked.

Gina closed her eyes. Memories flooded in of the ski boat, the laughter, her mother's smiling face and then…the collision. Gina went flying into the water, out of danger. Her parents hadn't been so lucky.

She shook her head and stared at the hands she'd placed in her lap. "No. I haven't had the courage. It's been almost ten years."

"So, why now?" Wade asked softly.

But she sensed he was really asking her, "Why me?" Why would she take her first boat trip with him? She'd been desperate for work she'd wanted to tell him. She needed the money and was determined to start her business again, without anyone's help this time. She'd been betrayed, but not destroyed. She wouldn't give up, and if that meant facing her fears, then so be it. She peered into a face filled with concern, an expression reminiscent of the sweet, caring Wade Beaumont she'd once known. "It's time, Wade. That's all."

Wade leaned back in the seat and put his arm around her. "That's not all. Tell me about the accident."

"I—I don't talk about it." She'd never really spoken about that day except with a support group that had really helped and understood what she'd been through. Losing both parents had been devastating enough, but to be the sole survivor of the crash that had taken four lives had been equally difficult. The result was major survivor guilt.

"Maybe you should. Maybe it'll help you overcome your fear of water."

She shook her head and gazed out upon the open sea. "I doubt that."

Wade took her hands in his and the look on his face, serious but earnest, urged her on. "Try, Gina. We're going to spend a week on an island surrounded by water. There'll be times we'll have to come back to the boat." He cast her a slight hint of a smile. "I can't have you fainting on me."

Gina peered into his eyes. They were warm with concern. But she wondered if that look was about keeping his personal assistant calm or if it was truly for her benefit.

He squeezed her hands gently, coaxing the words that she hadn't spoken to anyone but her support group. "It was Memorial Day weekend," she began, "and we never once thought to worry about drunk drivers on the water…"

Emotions rolled in the pit of Gina's stomach. She'd purged herself of her burden, sharing the events of that horrible day with Wade. He'd listened to her as she tried to communicate without tears, but at times her voice broke and she choked up. Wade sat there with a soothing arm around her shoulders, listening. And when the last words were out of her mouth, he thanked her for telling him.

"Are you feeling better?" he asked.

Gina nodded feeling a small sense of relief. "A little."

He stood and peered down at her. "You need to eat something."

"No," she said, placing a hand to her stomach. "No, I couldn't."

"If you don't want to eat, there's coffee down below." He glanced at the blue skies overhead then looked into her eyes as if deciding what was best for her. Then he took hold of her hand, guiding her up. "You look tired, Gina. Take a little rest. Get away from the water for a little while."

He spoke softly and his tone comforted. She thought she could fall for him again—if she hadn't sworn off men completely and if he would always look at her like he was now, without contempt and regret in his eyes. "Maybe I will go down below."

He walked her to the steps and turned, tugging

her close. She nearly bumped into his chest when the boat swayed. He steadied her with both hands on her shoulders then, with a slant of his head, brought his lips to hers. The kiss was brief and chaste and when it was over she gazed deeply into his eyes and smiled.

Wade looked off toward the horizon a moment then returned his focus to her face with narrowed eyes. His soft expression turned hard once again.

"Don't think I gained any satisfaction seeing fear in your eyes or hearing pain in your voice, Gina. I'm not that big a bast—"

Gina pressed her fingers to his mouth. "I know, Wade. You're not—"

He pulled her fingers from his lips. "I am. Make no mistake. But I draw the line at preying on another's weakness. Take that as fair warning."

Gina shuddered at Wade's harsh tone. He'd let her glimpse the man he'd once been, but only for a moment. The young man she'd fallen in love with was gone, she feared, forever. And she'd had everything to do with his demise. "Consider me fairly warned." She turned to walk down the stairs, feeling Wade's penetrating gaze following her every step of the way.

Wade guided the boat toward the mooring can in Avalon harbor on Catalina island and set about tying the lines to secure the boat from bow to stern. The trip had been uneventful, the weather calm, the sailing smooth. But his passenger had yet to return to the deck.

With the dinghy ready to take them ashore, Wade made his way to the cabin below. The galley was empty, the food he'd set out was untouched and there was no sign that Gina had even been there.

With a curious brow raised he walked to his master bedroom and bath, finding that room empty as well. He'd have guessed as much and smiled to himself, but his smile faded quickly when he finally found Gina, sprawled out on the bed in the guest-room.

"Gina," he said quietly.

When she didn't rouse, he entered the room and gazed down at her, lying across the bed, her hair in a tangle, the dark tresses half covering her beautiful face. The dress she wore rode up her thigh, the material exposing thoroughly tanned, shapely legs. She'd kicked off her shoes and made herself comfortable on the dark-russet bedspread. She looked peaceful and more tempting than a woman had a right to look. Hell, even her polished scarlet-red toenails turned him on.

Her eyes opened slowly, as though she'd sensed him watching her. With a sleep-hazy sigh, she stretched her limbs, reminding him of a cat uncurling after a long sleep.

"Mmmm…Wade," she purred and continued that long slow sensual stretch while keeping those lazy half-lidded eyes on him.

God, she was sexy.

But deceitful, too, he reminded himself. He could scarcely believe he'd hired her. She was his em-

ployee now and one he wasn't sure he could trust.
But his brother Sam had vouched unconditionally
for her. "Give her a chance, Wade," he'd said. And
Wade had because of Sam's request. But the truth
was that if she'd walked into his office without the
benefit of his brother's recommendation, he would
have hired her anyway. They had unfinished business. Period.

"I'd love to join you, Gina," he said softly, meaning
every word, "but we've got a full day ahead of us."

"Oh!"

Gina bounced up from the bed, realizing where she
was and with whom. Wade enjoyed every second of
that bounce and struggled to keep his lust from
becoming visible. Wouldn't take much to throw all
rational thought out the porthole and spread his body
over hers.

"Sorry, Wade." She untangled the hair that had
fallen into her face. "I guess I fell asleep. The rocking of the boat…"

She bent to put her shoes on and treated him to a
luscious view. From his position, the dress barely
contained her full breasts when she leaned over.

"This is embarrassing," she said. "I've never
fallen asleep on the job."

"I won't hold it against you. Anytime you want
to slip into one of my beds, feel free."

Gina rose then and looked into his eyes. "Too
bad we have a full day ahead of us," she bantered
back, repeating his words.

Wade hid his amusement.

"Are we on the island?" she asked.

Wade shook his head. "Not yet. There's a little matter of a dinghy ride to the dock."

The sleep-induced rosy color drained from Gina's cheeks. "How far?"

"Not far," he said. "We'll be ashore in less than five minutes."

Gina groaned and Wade almost felt sorry for her. "That's five minutes too long."

"Gina, you're gonna have to trust me. I'll keep you safe."

She angled her chin and probed him with those dark sensual eyes. "Trust goes both ways, Wade. Do you trust me?"

Wade held her gaze for a moment then refused her an answer and walked out the door.

Trusting Gina had never been an option.

Four

Gina held her breath through most of the dinghy ride to the mainland. Wade glanced at her from time to time, but his primary focus was on getting the small boat to shore and mooring at the dock. Once there, he secured the dinghy and stepped off the boat with her suitcase, then reached for her hand. "You okay?"

Gina nodded. "I will be as soon as my legs stop trembling."

Wade glanced down and raised a brow. "They look fine to me," he said, with a gleam in his eyes. "Come on, let's get you settled into your room."

Gina got control of her legs once she'd reached solid ground. The sun shined in the clear-blue sky and children's laughter rang out from the nearby beach. Catalina island was a nest for summer travelers wishing to get away from the daily grind of the big city. The mainland, visible on a clear day, was just twenty-two miles away. As they walked along the sidewalk, Spanish influences surrounded them, marking some of the history of the island. She noted a lovely tiled fountain bubbling up with a cool spray in the middle of a circular paved drive. Wade stopped for a minute in front of the fountain.

"Santa Catalina was originally named after Saint Catherine, the patron saint of spinsters," he said. "Lucky for my company, the island is now a resort for lovers."

"So the developer wants the resort to be known as an elite honeymoon destination?" she asked.

Wade nodded. "Can't think of a better place locally. Most of the hotels have no phones and televisions in the rooms. People get real creative to entertain themselves. This whole island spells romance."

Gina nodded as they walked past a row of swaying palms, the gentle sea breeze blowing by, the scent of sand and surf filling her nostrils. She supposed for most people that potent scent meant fun and sun and time away from the hassles of everyday life, but a resort surrounded by water only reminded her of things she'd rather forget.

Within a minute they were at the quaint town of Avalon and Gina looked down a long avenue, which she deemed to be the main street of town. The shops

and cafés faced the water and swimsuit-clad vaca-
tioners swarmed them as others biked their way down
the street. The only other vehicles on the busy
thoroughfare were canopied golf carts. Wade continued to lead the way but soon stopped again, this time
at a hotel. Villa Portofino. "Here we are," he said. She
looked up to see a hotel with all the trademarks of Italy.

Gina nodded. "Nice."

"None better, unless you take a trip to Tuscany."

Gina eyed him carefully, wondering why he'd
picked such an expensive place for her to stay. This
was just business and she would remind him of that
again, if she had to. "So your hotel will have competition."

"Not at all. We plan to build a lavish honeymoon
resort with pools, tennis courts and a golf course.
The Portofino is a great little beachfront hotel. It
won't give us any competition at all. This is where
our employees stay when in town working on the
project. You won't be disappointed."

Disappointment was the furthest thing from her
mind when she entered the Bella Vista suite. True to
its name, the suite's wraparound balcony had a grand
view of the lush hillside as well as the Catalina harbor.
A king-size bed in the center of the room faced a
large built-in fireplace and a table for two adorned by
a vase filled with tropical flowers. The bath was full-
size and encased with fine Italian marble. The whole
suite was larger than her tiny guesthouse in Hollywood.

Wade set her bag down and walked to the window

to stare out at the harbor. He'd waved off the bellboy, insisting on bringing her up here himself. "It's a far cry from El Paso."

Gina sucked in her breath. What could she say to that? Wade had made something of himself, despite his father's meddling. He was his own man and he'd made the West Coast Triple B a success. Gina couldn't argue with that. "I liked El Paso, Wade. It was the best summer of my life."

He whipped around to stare into her eyes. "I thought so, too…once." His eyes hardened on that last word.

Gina remembered her final week in El Paso. Sarah had been gone during that time, traveling from Dallas to Austin with her mother to interview for teaching positions. Mr. Buckley had been busy at work and Gina had been left pretty much on her own.

After their work was done on their uncle's ranch, Gina would meet Wade and Sam for ice cream or a movie or just to talk. But before long, it was only Wade coming around. They'd gotten close that last week, closer than she might have imagined, spending all of their time together. And they'd fallen in love over hot-fudge sundaes, hot summer walks and hot sizzling kisses.

No one had really known that their friendship had escalated. It hadn't been a secret, but they hadn't made any announcements either. Certainly Sarah hadn't known. Gina hadn't the time to confide in her and when she'd returned from those interviews,

Sarah had been edgy, anxious and unhappy, until she finally revealed her pregnancy to Gina and her parents.

Gina bit back her need to tell Wade the entire truth about Sarah. But destroying his friendship with Sarah wouldn't make up for what Gina had done. She hadn't trusted Wade and she *had* taken his father's money and left El Paso. Her reasons wouldn't matter to him, because Wade was a man who expected total loyalty. She had loved him back then, very much. But he wasn't the same man she'd fallen in love with. And she wasn't the same woman. The years had taught her hard lessons.

"What now?" she asked.

Wade became all business again. "Now? We have a late lunch meeting with James Robinique from the Santa Catalina Island Company. It'll take a few hours." He glanced around the room. "Enjoy yourself. Because after that, we'll be working our tails off."

Gina nodded. At least now they would get down to business. She never minded hard work. "How should I dress?"

Wade toured her body with a possessive eye. "Robinique is a lusty Frenchman with an eye for beauty. It won't matter if you wear a burlap sack, he'll still want to get you into bed."

Gina's mouth gapped open as Wade strolled out the door. Had that been a warning? Or had Wade coaxed her into coming here for an entirely different reason? She knew how important this project was to him, but enticing an island dignitary wasn't in her job description.

Gina couldn't believe it of Wade.

But the thought niggled at her far too much.

She grabbed a down pillow and flung it at the door Wade had just closed. The pillow smacked almost silently before falling to the floor, but it was enough to satisfy Gina's frustration.

"There, now I feel better," she muttered, wishing she had a burlap sack in her wardrobe. Because if she had one, she would surely have worn it just to spite Wade Beaumont.

A little later, Gina unpacked her bag, making sure to hang all of her clothes up carefully. She'd only brought one suitcase, packing enough clothes for the week, but she could make her wardrobe last two, if need be. She knew how to accessorize, how to mix and match and stretch out her clothes for maximum versatility. She prided herself on that. She loved design. She loved to create and one day, she vowed, her creativity would pay off.

A cooling breeze lifted her hair and she strolled to the wide French door Wade had opened, but instead of closing the door, she stepped outside. On a breath, she leaned against the balcony railing and gazed out at the ocean, tamping down shivers of fear, realizing that she'd crossed this ocean today with Wade by her side. She'd spent the better part of the trip below deck, but regardless of that, it was a first step to overcoming her fear.

Here she was on a small stretch of land, completely surrounded by water, working for Wade Beaumont. "Who would have guessed," she whispered into the breeze. She was living through the two scenarios she dreaded most. And the one man she hoped to never see again had orchestrated both.

Gina decided on taking a leisurely shower, luxuriating in the scented soaps, oils and body washes provided. Feeling rejuvenated, she sat down at the dressing table and brushed her long hair, deciding on another upswept do, this time leaving strands of hair down to frame her face. She used a little mascara on her eyes, highlighted the lids and put on a light shade of lipstick.

She decided on a conservative black pencil skirt and white-linen cuffed blouse to wear for the lunch meeting. Gazing in the mirror, she nodded in approval. This was business and, despite Wade's cutting remark, she wanted to appear every bit the professional.

An hour later when Wade knocked on her door, she was more than ready. "I'm all set," she said, opening the door.

Holding a briefcase in one hand and wearing equally professional dark trousers and a white shirt, he had a no-nonsense appearance: tall, dark, imposing. *Handsome.*

He made a quick sweep of her attire and she bit back a comment about burlap as he glanced down at her black-heeled sandals. "We have some walking to do."

Gina lifted one leg and twirled her foot. "These are the most comfortable shoes I own."

Wade arched a brow, taking time to stare at her toes. "Tell me that once we're back and I might believe you. Let's go."

She grabbed her purse, locked up her suite and Wade guided her downstairs with a hand to her back. "We'll go over the details once again about the Santa Catalina Island Company," he said as they walked along the streets.

Gina had read much about it in the reports, but Wade insisted on going over all pertinent information, more to reaffirm his knowledge, she believed, than to clue her in. He would do all the talking. Gina was there to take notes and provide any assistance Wade needed.

Wade explained once again how important this lunch was. The island company had been granted more than forty-thousand acres dedicated to conservation. Rarely did they agree to any building on the island. Anything proposed had to be in tune with the land and provide sanctuary for the wildlife and flora. The developer had sealed the deal, but Mr. Robinique needed to hear the plans directly from each contractor—whoever convinced him that the land would be best protected would gain the upper hand and have the best chance at winning the contract. Robinique's influence over the final proposal couldn't be discounted. Wade had three competitors, he reminded her, but only John Wheatley of Creekside Construction could truly compete with Triple B.

They climbed a hilly street to reach the snug

Harbor Inn and, once inside, Mr. James Robinique rose from his table to greet them. He shook hands with Wade and then smiled at Gina.

"This is my assistant, Miss Grady," Wade said.

Gina offered her hand and Robinique took it, clasping both of his over hers. "It's a pleasure," he said, his blue eyes never wavering.

Gina smiled at the good-looking Frenchman, taken aback by how young he appeared. From Wade's accounting, she'd expected a more mature man. But James Robinique appeared no older than her. He clasped her hand a little longer than she deemed necessary and slowly removed it from his. When she took her seat, the two men also sat down.

Once the meals had been ordered and served, the two men enjoyed healthy portions of halibut sautéed in wine sauce and conversed while Gina nibbled on her chicken salad. Wade drank beer on tap and Mr. Robinique sipped on pinot grigio. Gina opted for iced tea. She was on the clock and taking copious notes.

"Let me assure you that we have every intention of preserving the environment on the island. As you can see from the architectural layouts, there's a bird sanctuary on the grounds, not one tree will be downed and we have enhanced the outer perimeters with ponds and streams that will add to the island's beauty and invite the natural inhabitants."

With the layouts spread across the table, Robinique looked over the designs, making mental notes, nodding his head as Wade continued to make his case.

Gina jotted down his comments and questions, something Wade had asked her to do. Wade was nothing if not thorough and he wanted no stone left unturned.

Gina had to admire Wade's tenacity. He went after what he wanted without compromise. To hear him talk, you'd never guess that the resort—which would house seventy-five rooms, forty deluxe suites, six eloquent cottages, a horse-filled stable, three pools, tennis courts and a golf course—would disrupt the land in any way.

Yet, Mr. Robinique wasn't a pushover. He didn't appear completely convinced. He had specific, detailed concerns pertaining to the ninety acres in question. Wade admitted that he must do one more survey of the land before he could satisfy those questions.

Robinique agreed to meet with him later in the week, suggesting that Wade make use of the nearby stables to go over the entire acreage.

When Wade nodded in agreement, Robinique glanced at Gina. She had stopped writing and he spoke directly to her with just a hint of a French accent. "What do you think of all this, Miss Grady?" With a wave of his hands, he gestured to the plans.

"I think Mr. Beaumont and the staff at Triple B have worked diligently to try to satisfy both the developer and your company."

He kept his focus on her and smiled. "And I think Mr. Beaumont has a loyal employee."

Gina lifted her lips.

Wade kept his gaze tightly fastened to Robinique.

"Tell me, Miss Grady, are you through now, taking all those notes?"

Gina glanced at Wade. He nodded and she slipped the notepad into the briefcase. "Yes, I think so."

"Then your work is done for the day?"

"I'm not sure." She looked at Wade.

"If you are satisfied with the presentation, then I would say that our work is done for now," Wade offered. "But we will meet again later in the week."

"Then, we are finished," Robinique said, "unless you would care for coffee and dessert?"

Wade shook his head and looked at Gina. She too, shook her head. "No, thank you."

When Robinique stood, Wade took his cue and the two men shook hands. "I'll call you soon," Wade said, lifting his briefcase.

"I will expect your call," James Robinique replied, then turned to Gina. "Excuse me, Miss Grady" he began, his eyes a striking blue when focused solely on her, "but I cannot let you go without offering you our island hospitality. Would you care to join me for a drink later this evening?"

Gina felt Wade's eyes on her. He had a way of doing that, blatantly watching her with those intense-green eyes. But it was the charming blue eyes on a man with impeccable manners that had caught her off guard. Wade's words from earlier today flitted through her mind.

Lusty Frenchman.
Burlap sack.

Get you into bed.

James Robinique was certainly charming, but Gina wasn't interested in him. At one time in her life, she might have agreed to spend some time with the handsome man. Now all she wanted was to do a good job. She was here on business and she needed to keep her head in the game. She opened her mouth to answer, but Wade beat her to it.

"I plan to keep Gi-Miss Grady busy most of the night...*working.*" One side of Wade's mouth quirked up.

James Robinique blinked his eyes, then darted a glance her way before looking at Wade with a hint of envy. "I see. You are very dedicated then."

Wade nodded. "This project is important to my company."

Robinique gazed at Gina again, this time with more discerning eyes. "Yes, I can see that."

Gina's face flamed but, lucky for her, she'd always been able to hide her embarrassment under her olive complexion. Inside, she fumed. Wade had practically announced that they were lovers and all three of them knew it.

Nothing was further from the truth. Despite her need for job security, she couldn't let Wade get away with this. "I'm sorry, Mr. Beaumont, but I must take some personal time today. I've suddenly developed a terrible headache."

Blinding anger offered up the courage she needed to march out the front door of the restaurant and never look back.

* * *

Gina walked along the main streets of town until her feet ached, her anger ebbed and her heart had stopped racing like she'd just run a marathon. She peeked into shops but had no urge to stop. When tourists smiled at her she didn't smile back. She felt trapped on this island. Trapped in a job she shouldn't have taken—one she couldn't afford to lose.

She'd been out for two hours, enough time to simmer her hot Irish-Italian temper. She headed back to the hotel, contemplating a quiet night with a good book. As soon as she entered her suite, she kicked off her shoes. One flipped up and back hitting the wall behind her, the other slid across the floor to meet with another pair of shoes—a pair of *man's* shoes.

She looked up.

"Where the hell have you been?" Wade's angry voice startled her. He glared at her, arms folded, his face as firm and set as his tone.

"What are you doing in here?" she asked, none too pleased to find her boss invading her private space. "How dare you show up in my room like this!"

"You're on company time, Miss Grady. And this is a company suite."

"Oh, no. No way, Wade. This is my room and while I'm on this island, you have no right entering it without my permission. You're not paying me enough to…to—"

Wade stepped closer, until he was nearly in her

face, his green eyes, holding hers, his voice menacing. "Sue me."

Gina blinked. Anger she'd ebbed earlier rose up again with striking force. She turned her back on him, opened the front door and spoke with a quiet calm she didn't know she possessed. "Get out."

Wade strode to the door and, staring into her eyes, shoved it shut. "No one walks out on me, Gina. And no one dismisses me."

"You're so wrong. Maybe I can't throw you out of here, but I've already dismissed you." On shaky legs, she moved away from the door, away from him.

"What's got you so riled up anyway?"

Gina twirled around. Was he serious? Didn't he know how he had portrayed their relationship? "You deliberately let Robinique believe we were lovers, Wade. You staked your claim, though nothing's further from the truth. But more than that, you had no right to make that decision for me."

"Sleeping with Robinique would compromise the company."

He *was* serious. He'd actually thought she would— Furious, Gina calmed herself and took a different approach. "Quite the contrary, Wade," she began with a slow easy smile, "if I slept with him, the company would only benefit."

Wade couldn't really argue with that, though it galled him just thinking about Gina with James Robinique. Visions of making love to Gina, her soft pliant body meshed with his as they laid down on a soft cushion of hay, were never far from his mind. He remembered her, every inch of her, all too well. That night in El Paso had been magical. Though not experienced, Gina had pleased and pleasured him like no other woman had. "So, you're willing to take one for the team, so to speak?"

Her dark espresso eyes turned black as ink. She stood barefooted, hands on hips, looking at him with defiance. Only the king bed separated them and Wade's thoughts turned to it and how making love to her here would be on a soft mattress and silky sheets.

Gina's voice was deceptively calm, but the fury in her eyes gave her away. "I came here to work with you. Whether you believe me or not, I can be trusted. And if you'd given me the chance, you'd have seen me refuse Mr. Robinique's offer. I have no intention of sleeping with him or any other man. So no, I wouldn't have taken one for the team, Wade. Not like that. Now, please, it's been a long day. If there's nothing else you need from me, I'd like you to leave."

Wade stood his ground. He'd never trust Gina again, but he felt great satisfaction knowing that she would have refused Robinique. Though she'd been wrong on one account. She would sleep with one man while on this island. "Sorry, sweetheart, but you're forgetting who's the boss. And there is something else I need from you. I wasn't lying to Robinique when I said we'd be working into the night."

Gina's ire seemed to vanish. "Oh?"

Wade headed for the door. "We have a dinner meeting in exactly two hours. Be ready when I pick you up."

Gina stood there with a confused look on her face, her eyes softening, her rigid body relaxing. He glanced down at her red toenails and had never wanted a woman more.

Wade whipped the door open and exited.

Before he told her what he really needed from her.

The dinner meeting, held at a small eatery on Avalon's main street boasting buffalo milk, ended after ten o'clock. Gina had eaten quickly and immediately returned to taking notes. Wade had set up this dinner with local shop owners and proprietors to gain their support and trust, to get to know them, to assure them that if Triple B won the bid, their workers would add to the economy and not cause any trouble. Gina learned from day one that Catalina island thrived on the tourist trade. It was essential that there be no unsavory incidents and no bad press on the island. Wade was smart enough to know that, to understand their concerns.

When all was said and done, Wade escorted her outside and, as they headed toward her hotel suite, he asked. "How do you think that went?"

"By their own admission, not one of the other builders had approached them. Your assurances went a long way. I'd say you scored points."

Wade nodded. "I want to be on friendly terms when we win the bid. Our crews are the best, but get a bunch of men working in a confined area for too long and that might spell trouble. They needed to know I'd do everything in my power to keep things running smoothly."

"I think you convinced them." Wade wasn't just blowing smoke. Gina really believed he meant what he said. Nine years ago, she would never have believed that the roughriding rancher with the sweet nature would become such an astute businessman. She never pictured him in that role. Yet here he was, talking the talk, making the deals. Gina shook her head.

Wade caught the slight movement. "What?"

"Nothing, really. It's nothing."

Wade was silent for a while, then before they reached her hotel, he stopped. "I could use a drink. There's a nightclub up the street known for their tropical drinks. Care to join me?"

Gina hesitated. A nightcap sounded wonderful. She'd had a tumultuous day. She was physically exhausted but the idea of relaxing with a piña colada and some good music sounded great. "I bet the music's real loud."

"Probably," Wade replied honestly.

Gina nibbled on her lower lip. "It's probably crowded."

"Without a doubt."

"Am I on the clock?" she asked. Looking into Wade's beautiful green eyes what she really wanted to know was if his request had been a demand of the job or a simple invitation.

Wade shook his head. "Not at all. I don't like to drink alone, but if it's not what you—"

"I could use a drink, too."

"Great. Let's go," he said, with a pleased look on his face. They strolled up a slightly inclined street and, somewhere along the way, Wade twined his fingers with hers and they entered the nightclub hand in hand.

For Gina, it felt as natural as breathing.

Five

"I want to make love to you," Wade whispered in her ear, his warm breath combined with those softly spoken words caused havoc to her nerves and brought tingles to her toes.

With her arms wrapped around his neck, their bodies brushing, swaying to the jazz band's bluesy sensual ballad, Gina rested her head on his shoulder. After two piña coladas, her brain was fuzzy, but not fuzzy enough to disregard what was happening between them. She was fully aware of what Wade wanted. "It's not in my job description," she whispered back softly.

She felt Wade's smile. It was difficult not to feel the same arousing sensations, not to succumb to his body heat or the pressing evidence of that desire. Gina wanted him, too.

"I told you before, you're not on the clock, Gina."

Wade dropped his hands down lower on her back, his fingers splaying across her derriere. He made soft caressing circles as he drew her closer. "Remember how it was between us, Gina? It can be that way again."

She shouldn't allow him such liberties. The fact remained that he was still her boss. They had a job to do here on the island. But the sensations swept through her with blinding force. His touch heated her, his words enticed her and his hard body stirred her softer one. She raised her head from his shoulder to look into his eyes.

It was a mistake.

Wade's intense gaze blazed into hers, before his lips came down in a soul-searing kiss, right there on the crowded, smoky dance floor. They kissed. And kissed.

Gina's body ignited, but dire warnings fanned the flames quickly. She couldn't allow Wade in. Not again.

She shoved at his chest and pulled away from him, her body swamped with heat, defying her reasoning. "I didn't come here for this," she breathed out. "It's not a good idea."

Wade reacted immediately. "I can't think of a better one."

Rather than make a scene right there in the nightclub, Gina moved off the dance floor. She walked outside, letting the cool sea breezes clear her head. Wade was beside her instantly. "You're still a liar, Gina."

Gina scoffed and began walking down the street. "Your bedside manner needs improving, Wade."

Wade kept pace, his hand placed possessively on her back. "There's not a damn thing wrong with my bedside manner. And you'll find that out as soon as you stop lying to yourself and admit what you really want."

Gina heaved a big sigh, her head in as much turmoil as her quaking body. "What I *want* is to go to bed. Alone."

Wade curled a hand around her neck, bringing her face close, as he came around to block her from walking past him. She was forced to look into those smoldering green eyes.

They stood under the moonlit night sky with twinkling stars overhead, right outside the entrance of her hotel. "Sorry, sweetheart, but what you want is for me to crawl up inside your sheets, strip you naked and rock your world."

Gina's mouth opened. Then closed.

"It's going to happen, Gina. Bank on it."

He left her standing on the front steps of the hotel, captivated by the steamy image swirling around in her head, more angry than she ever remembered being and wishing that, more than anything, Wade Beaumont had been wrong.

Wade dressed in a pair of Wranglers, faded not by the manufacturer, but by hard work and long wear, a plaid shirt and his Stetson. He put on his boots and left *Total Command* to pick up Gina this morning.

Although clothes didn't make the man, Wade was comfortable in these, the old standbys, the worn leather of his boots and the soft cotton of his shirt reminding him of his time at Uncle Lee's ranch in El Paso. He wasn't that young man anymore. Time, with all the hardships, heartaches and headaches, had a way of changing a man.

His heart had hardened. And he knew it. He was relentless when he wanted something. Maybe that much of his old man had rubbed off on him. Wade wanted two things. He wanted to win the bid on the Catalina project and he wanted Gina.

Neither one would escape him. He would see to that.

He knocked on her door at precisely 8:00 a.m.

When she didn't answer, he knocked again, harder.

"Are you looking for me?"

Wade whipped around in the hallway and caught Gina's unfettered expression. She hadn't recognized him, that much was obvious. And once she had that genuine look vanished.

"Oh," she said, standing there, her breaths coming quickly, with sweat on her forehead, dressed in killer shorts and a white spandex top. "Wade, I didn't—"

"Do you run?"

A quick smile curled her lips. "I try."

They stood silent for a moment, gazing at each other, but Wade couldn't miss Gina's probing eyes and those few rapid blinks as she took in his appearance, as if trying to figure out which man he really was: the fast, hard businessman or the easy, kind cowboy she'd once known.

The confusion in her eyes bothered him, so he ignored her expression and swept his gaze instead to her long legs, and tanned smooth skin. More leg than she'd allowed him lately. And as his gaze traveled upward, he noted her breaths coming fast and the spandex top unable to confine the swell of her breasts and the damned enticing tips of her erect nipples.

Her hair was pulled back in a ponytail. She looked sweaty and hot and sexy enough to have for breakfast.

"I thought I had an hour before going to the stables," she said, opening the door to her suite and entering.

Wade followed her inside. "You do, but we need to eat something first. I ordered room service. Breakfast will be here soon."

In a single fluid move, Gina pulled the elastic band from her hair and chestnut strands flowed onto her shoulders, framing her face. "Let me guess, last night you didn't want to drink alone and today you don't want to eat alone."

Wade shrugged off her comment as he tossed his hat onto her bed. "Doesn't figure for me to eat alone when I have a beautiful assistant at my disposal."

"I may be at your disposal in business, Wade, but that's the extent of it."

Again, he ignored her. "You look *hot.*"

Gina frowned. "I know. I'm hot and sweaty. I must look a mess." She ran her hand through her hair in an unconscious move that had Wade approaching her.

"Not a mess." He strode the rest of the distance separating them, facing her toe to toe. *"Sexy as hell."*

Gina blinked then captured his gaze as well as his meaning. She backed up a step, her tone filled with warning as she shook her head slightly. "Wade."

Wade reached for her waist, encircling his arms around her and pulled her close. A combination of female and salty scents drifted up as she looked at him with hesitation in her eyes.

"Don't fight it, honey." Wade swooped his mouth down and took her in a long, slow, deliberate kiss that had her molding her body to his. A little moan escaped her throat when Wade cupped her buttocks, pressing her to the juncture of his thighs.

She fit him perfectly. She always had. Immediate heat swamped him and his groin tightened envisioning her on the bed with him, just a few feet away. He'd wanted her, wanted *that* ever since she'd walked into his office a few days ago.

A knock at the door broke the moment.

Wade winced at the bad timing. And, as he tugged his mouth from hers, he whispered, "Room service." Wade had a notion to send the waiter packing and finish this. Just as he began to utter those commands, Gina backed away.

"I—I need a shower."

Wade glanced at her chest, the tempting swell of her breasts straining against her spandex top with her breathes coming hard again, only this time, he knew her fast breathing had nothing to do with the run she'd just taken. "So do I—a cold one."

Gina's gaze slipped down to his jeans, her eyes riveted below his waist.

Wade ground out a warning. "Don't tempt me, Gina."

"I never mean to."

That was the problem. Gina, just being Gina, was enough of a temptation. Didn't matter what she wore, how she looked, Wade found himself wanting her, no matter what. She was beautiful to him. That much hadn't changed. From the moment he'd set eyes on her almost ten years ago, he'd wanted her. Had to have her.

The only difference between now and then was that now he knew he'd have her but he'd never keep her.

The knock came louder this time, announcing, "Room service!"

Wade let out a deep sigh, restraining his desire. "I'll get the door. You get your shower."

Gina nodded and, without a word, entered the bathroom. After a second, he heard the decided click of the bathroom door's lock.

Gina mounted a bay mare, fitting herself as comfortably as she could on the saddle. It had been almost ten years since she'd ridden a horse. She'd been taught by the best; Mr. Buckley, Sarah and

Wade all had a hand in teaching her how to ride. But she was rusty and uncertain.

"Don't let her know you're nervous," Wade said, gripping the reins, holding the mare steady from the ground. Gina took a deep breath and nodded.

"You'd think a girl born and bred in Texas would know more about horses than how to hang onto the saddle horn."

Wade grinned. "You were from Austin. That doesn't count."

"Austin was full of horses." Gina tipped her chin up in defiance.

"Right. And you rode how many?"

Wade didn't wait for an answer. He handed her the reins, then swung his long legs up and over his saddle, mounting a tall dappled-gray mare. "Follow my lead. Loosen up on the reins and use only slight motions to guide the mare. You'll do fine."

"I can't take notes and ride. Why do you need me?"

"I need another pair of eyes."

Gina doubted that. She knew for certain that scores of Triple B's finest—from architects to financial accountants—had surveyed the property already.

"Ready?"

Gina squirmed once more in her saddle and adjusted the straw hat Wade had purchased in town for her. "Ready."

Wade made a soft sound to his mare and with just the slightest click of his boot heels, the horse took off. Gina's mare followed and they rode off the stable grounds and away from the road, heading further into the interior of the canyon.

Ten minutes later, Wade reined his horse to a stop. Saddle leather creaked when he turned around in his seat. "Take a look," he said.

Gina's gaze flowed in the direction he was pointing. They had steadily climbed and had come to a low rise that overlooked the entire town of Avalon and the crescent-shaped bay below. From this distance and under clear-blue skies, the ocean seemed less threatening with a throng of boats harbored in the stunning turquoise bay. "It's remarkable."

Wade agreed with a low grumble. "It's hard to believe this place once was home to pirates and trappers."

"Yes, but I can picture it, can't you? The wildness here, the untouched land and those men coming here, some for honest work, others to do harm or hide out."

Wade cast her a long thoughtful look, his eyes narrowing as if picturing it. "Yeah, I can see that," he said, his lips quirking in a distant smile, before turning back around.

Once again he *looked* like the Wade she'd known in El Paso, only more mature, stronger, more capable, if that were even possible.

"Not much longer now," Wade said, as they passed oaks and sage and tall limber stalks of sun-yellow and white poppies.

They met up with a road again and Gina saw the gates that led to a clearing. No Trespassing signs cordoned off the area.

Wade dismounted and used a key to unlock the chains on the gate before mounting his mare again. Gina followed him inside.

The clearing where the resort was to be built was anything but clear. Tall cottonwoods blocked the sun, natural formations jutted up from the earth and canyon walls provided the backdrop.

"The architects have done a great job in preserving most of what you see. We won't down these trees. They'll be a natural part of the landscape. Out there in the distance, a wildflower meadow allows just enough land to build the main hotel and facilities. About half a mile down the road there's a secluded cove that we'll utilize for special occasions and weddings. You name it. This is the first project I've been involved with where the land dictates the building, instead of the other way around. I think Robinique understands that."

Wade spurred his mare on. "Come on. I need to see it all one more time and get your opinion."

"I've seen the plans on paper, Wade. But it's hard for me to picture it. Seems like this place needs to stay untouched."

"*Nothing* stays untouched, Gina." He cast her a narrow-eyed look from under the brim of his Stetson. "I learned that lesson a long time ago."

"So as long as it's going to be *touched*, you might as well be the one doing the touching?"

Wade stared deeply into her eyes, capturing her and making her flinch from his intensity. "That's right."

Heat crept up Gina's neck. She wanted out of this conversation, knew she should let the comment go, but she couldn't. Wade had twisted her words and suddenly they weren't speaking about the land any longer. She fought her rising anger. "When did you become so ruthless?"

Wade's voice held contempt. "You know the answer to that."

Gina slumped in the saddle. Telling him the truth now wouldn't do any good. Wade had changed. He was a man walking in the shadow of his father. He was just as driven, just as bitter. Getting involved with him again would be a big mistake. She'd already had a bad relationship with one unscrupulous man and she feared Wade Beaumont, too, would only use her then toss her aside.

Gina kept Sarah's secret close to her heart. It wasn't her secret to divulge anyway. If Sarah wanted Wade to know the truth, then she would tell him in her own time. Long-standing friendships were at stake here and Gina wanted no part in destroying Sarah's relationship with Wade. Gina was the outsider and she would always remain so. "We'd be better off just sticking to business, Wade."

Wade cocked his head and sent her a crooked smile. "That's all I was talking about. Business."

Gina's temper rose with lightning speed. There was no stopping the rage within her. She silently cursed Wade and his infuriating hold on her. She needed to get away from him. She kicked her mare's flanks just as a wild hawk swooped down from a cottonwood. The horse reared up in fright—nearly tossing Gina from the saddle—then her front hooves landed hard onto the ground and the mare took off running.

Startled, the reins dropped from Gina's hands. She grabbed for the saddlehorn, bouncing on the seat as the mare raced across the meadowland. Her hat flew from her head as she hung on.

She heard Wade's commands from behind, knew he was racing behind her, trying to catch up. Gina held on for dear life. Her shoes came out of the stirrups from the turbulent ride. She lost her balance in the saddle and her grip on the horn. Within seconds, she was tossed off the horse.

She hit the ground hard.

Dazed from the fall, she heard Wade's footsteps fast approaching. And then he was leaning down beside her with fear in his eyes and a voice filled with gentle condemnation. "Damn it, Gina. You're always running away."

Six

With her head pounding, her body twisted and the air knocked out of her, Gina squinted into the morning sun. Wade moved to obstruct the light, his tone fierce but his hands gentle as he touched and surveyed her body for injuries. "Did you hit your head?"

She gazed into his eyes as his fingers searched for a bump. "I have a hard head."

"Tell me about it," he muttered, yet the softness in his eyes belied his tone. When he didn't find a bump on her head, his hands traveled to her face, gently turning her right to left, searching for injury. "Can you untwist your body?"

Gina did exactly that. She straightened her form

then winced. "I'm sore, but at least everything's moving."

He frowned and spoke quietly, "The fall won't really hit you until tomorrow."

Gina looked up into his eyes. She liked what she saw there. In an unguarded moment, Wade let down his defenses and she witnessed the depth of his compassion. "You mean I have aches and pains to look forward to?"

"Remember when I tried to break Rocket? That horse wouldn't give in. He must have thrown me a dozen times."

Gina nodded, recalling Wade's determination to break the wild stallion his uncle Lee had captured in the mountains. After several bronc-busters had tried, his uncle Lee had just about given up and had been ready to turn the stallion loose. But Wade had been more stubborn than the stallion and had finally tamed the beast. "I remember that you had trouble walking the next day." Then it dawned on her. Slightly panicked, she tried to rise up. "You're not saying I'm going to feel like that?"

Wade placed a calming hand to her shoulder. "Hold still, honey."

In one grand sweeping movement, Gina was lifted up into Wade's arms. She automatically roped her arms around his neck. He carried her to the shade of an ancient oak.

He felt solid and warm and, when he peered down at her, she couldn't miss the concern in his beautiful green eyes.

"You're not as tough as you let on," she whispered near his ear. "Sometimes, I see the man you were in El Paso, Wade."

"I don't think he exists anymore, Gina." Wade pitched his Stetson and Gina watched the hat land near her mare's hooves. It was so telling, so obvious what that toss of the hat meant. Wade didn't want to go back. He'd moved into the role of a high-powered executive and was comfortable there.

She let out a quiet sigh. "A girl can hope, can't she?"

Wade stared into her eyes for a long moment and nodded then lowered down to sit against the base of the oak, keeping Gina firmly in his arms and on his lap. "Are you hurt? Do you feel dizzy?"

She shook her head, "I'm not hurt at all. My head's fine. You can let me up now."

"I can't," he said.

Her brows lifted. "Can't?"

"Don't want to, won't."

He smiled, right before his lips touched hers. The brush of his mouth over hers sent warm comforting shivers throughout her body.

She wound her arms tighter about his neck and he deepened the sweet kiss, coaxing her mouth open. From there, Wade took complete control, mating their tongues in a slow fiery seduction while his hand stroked her face then her throat. Gentle fingers traveled lower, unfastening the top buttons of her blouse.

Wade had her in his arms, at his mercy. Gina

couldn't fight her desire any longer. She was where she wanted to be. The Wade she'd known was still there, inside, somewhere in the soft caress of his eyes, in the caring way he held her and in the coaxing brush of his lips. She wanted Wade Beaumont to return. She wanted the man she'd once loved. She'd do anything to bring him back to her.

He slipped his hand inside her blouse. She moaned when he touched her breasts, remembering those fingers, gentle yet rough against her skin. She strained against him. He took more, easing her bra down, cupping her, flicking her nipple until she moaned louder, feeling the pulse of his erection against her thigh.

When he broke off the kiss, they looked deeply into each other's eyes. "Definitely feeling dizzy now," she whispered softly.

Wade smiled again and spoke in a low, raspy voice. "You want me."

It wasn't a question but a statement of fact. One she couldn't deny. "Yes."

Wade kissed her again and palmed her breast until spiraling heat curled up from her belly.

"This is a long time coming, Gina."

He pressed her down lower on his lap and, leaning over her, he slipped his hand under the waistband of her jeans, his fingers trekking slowly, teasing, tempting, until finally he reached her.

Gina welcomed him. His touch, the stroking of his fingers as they kissed, brought damp moist heat and an ecstasy she'd only known in his arms.

Suddenly, Wade froze, his head shooting up and he muttered a foul curse.

"What is it?" Gina asked, stunned by his quick abandonment.

"Security jeep. Coming from down the road. They must have seen the gate unlocked."

He lifted her off him and together they stood facing each other, Gina's clothes as disheveled as her mind.

"Get dressed," he said. "I'll go meet them. Explain who we are."

No words came. She could only nod.

Wade plucked his hat from the ground, yanked it onto his head and strode over to his horse. Before mounting, he turned to her with deep regret in his eyes, as he watched her button her blouse. "One of these days I'm going to make love to you in a damn bed."

Wade escorted Gina back to town, leaving her in front of the hotel. She'd been quiet on the ride back to the stables and then, as they walked back to the hotel, she hadn't said more than a few sentences. Wade wasn't in the mood for talking either. He'd had a few choice words for the security guards who needed convincing that he wasn't a trespasser. Their interruption had cost him. His desire for Gina had gone unsatisfied and that made him want her all the more.

It irritated the hell out of him how much he wanted her. She couldn't be trusted and he'd never forgive her for her betrayal, so why wasn't he satisfied with all the other women he'd had in his life?

"Take a few hours to rest. We have a late lunch meeting. I'll go to the boat and do some work. I'll be back later to pick you up."

Gina nodded, but kept her eyes from meeting his. "Okay."

Wade cupped her chin and forced her to look at him. "Are you up for it?"

She shot him a look of defiance. "I came here to work, Wade." She backed away, releasing his hold on her. "So yes, I'm up for it. But back there, that was a mistake. We've both changed. We're not the same people we were when we knew each other in El Paso. You're paying me to be your personal assistant. I don't believe sleeping with the boss is in my job description."

Wade tamped down rising anger. "*That* had nothing to do with business or the fact that I'm your boss. As I recall, you said yes and couldn't wait for me to get into your pants."

Gina's dark eyes went wide. She lifted her hand and Wade warned her with a searing glance not to even try it. When she lowered her hand, she spoke with quiet calm, her words more potent than any slap to the face. "I thought I saw an inkling of the man you once were, Wade. The man I wanted above all else, the man who was kind and generous and caring. But I was mistaken, you're *nothing* like him."

Wade jammed his hands in the back pockets of his jeans, watching her spin around and walk into the hotel lobby. Her words stung but he wouldn't be played for a fool ever again.

No matter how much he wanted her.

* * *

Wade poured himself a whiskey on the rocks, something that always soothed his bad temper, and took a seat at his desk. He let the mellow rocking of the boat and the fresh sea breeze calm him for several minutes before opening his e-mail account. He punched in his password and viewed more than a dozen messages forwarded to him from Triple B.

As he went through half of them, all having to do with the Catalina project, Wade came upon one message he hadn't expected, from Sarah Buckley.

He hadn't spoken with Sarah in over six months. They'd always remained friends, but ever since that episode with Gina years ago, their relationship hadn't been quite the same. He'd left El Paso shortly after that tumultuous summer to work at Triple B with his father. Maybe his imagination was in overdrive, but whenever he had visited his uncle and aunt in El Paso, he'd also made a stop in to see the Buckleys and, oddly, they'd been slightly distant, polite but not as friendly as he remembered. And Sarah, too, had seemed more cautious with him.

He punched in and opened the e-mail.

Wade, I know you're out of town, but it's important that you call me when you return. We need to talk.
Always,
Your friend,
Sarah

Wade sipped his drink, staring at the message for a moment, making a mental note to call Sarah once he returned to Los Angeles. Right now, he had enough to deal with, Gina being right up there on his list.

He realized his approach with Gina had been completely wrong. She wasn't an easy female to figure out but he did know that when she was backed into a corner, she came out fighting. Though she was as headstrong and volatile as she was beautiful, Wade wouldn't let her get away this time around. She had become nearly as important as the Catalina Project and both were challenges he fully intended to win. He finished his drink, took a quick shower and changed into different clothes. Before meeting Gina at the hotel, he had one important errand to run.

Gina glanced at the digital clock on the bed stand. It was ten minutes after two and Wade was late. It wasn't like him to be late for a meeting.

She glanced at her reflection in the framed beveled mirror, straightening out her tan skirt and cream knit shell top. She tossed the short tailored jacket she'd donned minutes ago onto the bed and headed to the wraparound balcony for a breath of fresh air.

Her nerves had been wrought ever since she'd come to this island. The trip over here in Wade's yacht had nearly done her in and she hadn't thought things could've gotten any worse. But they had.

She didn't know where she stood with Wade. He was her boss, that was a given. He wanted to be her lover. That's where it all got confusing. She knew enough not to get involved with him romantically, yet when he kissed her and touched her tenderly, memories flooded in, sweet hot wonderful memories of the times they had shared in the past. Gina had succumbed to him earlier today and the heat of his touch still sizzled on her lips and other highly sensitive parts of her anatomy. Wade had left his mark on her body.

A light-hearted tap on the door surprised her. She strode the distance wondering who it could be. Certainly Wade's knock had always been more commanding. When she opened the door to her suite, she stood in awe, looking at a smiling Wade, dressed in khaki shorts and a tan polo shirt, black beach sandals on his feet.

"Our meeting was cancelled," he said, walking in holding a shopping bag. "I figured we both could use some down time."

"Down time?" Gina asked, confused by Wade's uncharacteristic light mood.

"Yeah, you know…relax, soak up some sun, enjoy the beach."

Gina stared at Wade. "That sounds nice," she fibbed. The last place she could relax was staring out at the fathomless ocean. "But I'm afraid I didn't bring 'down time' clothes with me. Sorry, you'll have to go it alone." She sent him a small smile.

Wade lifted up the bag. "That's why I brought this."

Gina watched him set the bag on her king-size bed. "Oh, I was hoping that was lunch."

Wade shot her a sweeping glance, his eyes raking in her body from top to bottom. "Depends on how you look at it."

"What? What did you bring me?" Gina walked over to the white bag and tossed the contents onto the bed. Swimsuits, sarongs and fancy rhinestone flip-flops scattered. Gina lifted up a pure-white dazzling bikini. "A thong?" She turned to face him. "Not on your life."

Wade laughed. "I had to try." He gestured to the others. "What about the black one?"

Gina eyed him cautiously, before picking it up and scanning it over. The bikini had a tad more material than the thong, she noted. She shook her head. "You don't know my size."

Wade stepped closer to her and looked into her eyes. He spoke softly, with confidence. "I know your body, Gina. They'll fit."

Heat rushed up, warming her throat and blistering her face. Once again she thanked the Almighty for her olive complexion. At least she could hide her blush from Wade, if nothing else. She set the suit down. "I'd really rather stay in."

Wade folded his arms across his middle. "Okay, we'll stay in." He glanced at her then the bed. "What do you suppose we can do in here all afternoon?"

Gina flinched. "I wasn't inviting you."

Wade took a seat on the sofa, his arm spread along the top cushion. "Gina, what are you afraid of? We'll go down, have lunch at a café, then relax on the beach for a few hours."

"You know I don't like the water."

"You traveled twenty-two miles over that water to get here."

"I know. I'm dreading the trip back." Just the thought brought shivers.

Wade pointed to the clothes on the bed. "Try the red one, Gina. It's a one-piece."

Gina glanced at it and frowned. "With more cutouts than Swiss cheese."

"You noticed that, too?"

Wade didn't even try to hide his amusement. "Come on, Gina. You must be starving by now."

Gina's stomach rumbled quietly. Thankfully, Wade didn't seem to hear. She was hungry and it seemed the only way to get Wade out of her hotel room was to leave with him. "Okay, fine. I'll wear the red one."

Gina grabbed the swimsuit, a multicolored sarong and sparkling rhinestone flip-flops and stomped into the bathroom, ignoring Wade's satisfied chuckle from the sitting area.

She knew he'd be right. Everything he bought would fit her.

Perfectly.

Gina sipped her piña colada, the coconut-and-rum tropical drink sliding cold and smooth down her throat. Wearing the cherry-red swimsuit underneath the sarong cover-up, she faced Wade from her seat at the beachfront café, surprised at his casual demeanor. He'd dominated the conversation, opening up to her about his time at Triple B working with his father, learning the business, then taking over after his father died and Sam remarried and started a new life at Belle Star Stables. He'd filled her in on his life from the time he left El Paso to the present. Of course, she was certain that he'd left out choice bits about his love life and he'd skirted the issue about their onetime hot and steamy relationship.

If he'd wanted her to relax, he'd succeeded. The two empty piña colada glasses in front of her might have had something do with it as well, but Gina wouldn't look a gift horse in the mouth.

"So what about you? What did you do once you landed in Los Angeles?" he asked, his tone light, his eyes holding nothing but curiosity.

Gina had always wanted Wade to understand what her life had been like before and after she met him. There had been so many things left unsaid. Perhaps now was the time, after all this time, to come clean, at least partly. She'd always wanted Wade's trust and maybe this was the first step in gaining it back.

"I'd always liked Los Angeles. Sarah and I roomed at UCLA for four years together. We were girls from two different worlds. Though I was raised in Austin, my parents were city folks. They owned a small Italian restaurant. My mother was a terrific cook."

"As I recall, so were you."

"Thank you. It was a family-run operation. I worked there until I left for college."

"And after college, when you left El Paso, what did you do?"

Gina peered at Wade. He'd just polished off a sandwich and was working on the fries and his second beer. Because she didn't find any sign of resentment, any hint of a trap, she continued. "I looked for work and did some odd jobs here and there. Nothing too stimulating, but all the while I'd been working on clothing designs. That's when I realized I'd probably wasted four years of my life in college. I should have been following my heart. I entered the Fashion Institute and loved every minute of it. When I got out, I ventured into my own business. Or at least, I tried."

"What do you mean, you tried?" Wade asked. "What happened?" He plucked another fry up and shoved it into his mouth.

Gina took a deep breath and surged on. "I didn't have any money, so I took on a partner. A man. He seemed to have more business sense than me, some really good ideas. We took out loan after loan to fund our venture. I…trusted him."

Wade took a pull from his beer. "Mistake?"

"Big, big—huge—mistake."

Wade set his beer down and leaned in, his elbows braced on the table now. "I'm listening."

"He stole my designs and every bit of money we'd borrowed. I have no idea where he is or what happened to him."

Wade studied her a moment as if sorting something out in his mind. "Were you involved with him?"

Gina paused, hating to admit this to Wade. She'd been such a fool. "Yes. He was charming and so easy to be with…a charming con man."

Wade sat back in his seat, looking at her. "I get it now. Why you took the job working for me."

"I'm in debt, Wade. I owe a lot of people a lot of money."

"You shouldn't have to pay it all back."

Gina bit her lip, and swallowed. "Some of the loans were in my name only—a good many of them."

Wade nodded and had her gratitude for not telling her what a gullible fool she'd been.

"I plan to repay every loan. There isn't anything I won't do to clear my name. I still want my dream. I still have the designs in my head. I know I can do it, but first I need to clean up my debts."

He eyed her now, holding her gaze. He was a wealthy affluent man and her debts might seem trivial to him, but to her, the thousands she owed were monumental. "How much are we talking about here?"

Gina shrugged and smiled. "You don't want to know. It doesn't matter. Like I said, I'll do whatever it takes to get out from under all my debt. Then I plan to start GiGi Designs on my own. I'm determined."

Wade shot her a look of admiration and she wondered where that had come from. Nervous and uncomfortable from his perusal, Gina changed the subject. "Are you through with lunch?"

He smiled. "Do you see anything left on my plate?"

"Then I guess we should get the relaxing on the beach and soaking up the sun over with."

Wade stood, tossed some cash onto the table and took her hand in his. "It's hardly cruel and unusual punishment."

Gina only smiled at the comment, but for her that's exactly how it seemed. She doubted she'd ever be comfortable sitting on the beach just steps from the ocean.

Ten minutes later, they were lying against rented sand chairs, lathered in sunscreen, watching children play in the water. Wade's eyes were closed under his dark sunglasses, his chest bare and his long lean legs stretched out along a beach towel. He looked magnificent.

When one little girl slipped and went under a wave, Gina rose up and gasped. "Oh no."

Wade glanced up, noting Gina's distress. They both watched the child lift up from the water, dripping wet, her face animated and her joyous laughter ringing through the noisy beach.

Relieved, Gina sank back down, trying hard to control her irrational fear. It was enough that she couldn't stand the water, but she should be able to see others enjoying themselves without thinking the very worst. Without those terrifying flashes of memory hitting her.

"Come on, Gina. We're going for a walk."

Gina hadn't noticed Wade rise up from his chair to stand over her. He blocked the sun, peering down at her through those dark shades. "Where?"

"Along the beach."

Gina shook her head fiercely. "No, thank you."

"It'll do you good."

"I...can't, Wade." Didn't he understand her fear? She explained to him that she hadn't stepped foot in a swimming pool—or any body of water—since the accident. Her bathtub days were over as well—she was unable to sit in a tub full of water for any length of time. Sitting just feet from the bay did enough to jangle her nerves.

He reached for her hand. "I think you can. Trust me, on this." He removed his sunglasses to peer deeply into her eyes. "Come on. You'd be doing me a favor."

"A favor?" she asked incredulously. "How so?"

He swept his gaze over her, then zeroed in on her breasts, which were nearly popping out from his most conservative choice of swimsuit. Conservative for a showgirl, that is. "It's torture sitting next to you wearing that thing. Making out on a public beach isn't my style. So do me a favor and take a walk with me. I need the distraction."

Gina laughed, despite her fear. "You're such a liar, Wade. I know what you're trying to do."

"Don't be so sure that I'm lying." Then he leaned down to within a breath of her. Her gaze flowed over his strong, muscled chest, then up to his face, the hot gleam in his green eyes. "And don't tempt me. I'd rather be on a private beach with you, but this just might have to do."

Gina didn't believe him for a second, yet his

powers of persuasion couldn't be denied. "Okay, let's go for a short walk."

Wade nodded, slipped his sunglasses on and took her hand. "Let's go."

The short five-minute walk Gina had hoped for ended up being a thirty-minute stroll along the beach with Wade doing all the talking, *all the distracting*. He held her hand and she knew this time it was to lend moral support rather than any need he had for intimacy. Once they reached a secluded cove, far away from the loud boisterous beach crowd, Wade stopped by the water's edge and turned her by the shoulder to look into his eyes.

"Just stand here." He took both of her hands now and held on. They faced each other, her back to the ocean. "Keep looking at me."

Gina held her breath, her bare feet digging into the hot sand. "If you're trying to torture me, you're doing a fine job."

"I'm trying to help. The surf's coming up."

Gina flinched.

Wade held her firm. "I've got you. Don't move. Just let it wash over your toes. Gina, look at me!"

She did. She looked into his eyes. This was his best revenge. If he meant her harm, wanted to hurt her, this was the way. But for once, Gina gave him the benefit of the doubt. She believed he was sincere, wanting to help. And the only reason she came up with was that Wade couldn't stand to see weakness in others. He couldn't relate. He had no clue how hard it was for her to stand on this beach and give him her full trust.

Water lapped over her feet.

She closed her eyes and fought from running onto dry land. The chill hit her first, then the moisture as her feet dug in again, this time into cool wet sand. It lasted only seconds and once the water ebbed she opened her eyes.

Wade was there, watching her, still holding her hands tight.

"You did it." There was admiration in his voice. "I know it wasn't easy."

"Can I go back to the hotel now?"

Wade smiled. "Once isn't enough. It never is with you."

And then he brought her closer, crushing his lips to hers, lifting her onto the tips of her feet.

She barely felt the next wave as it curled around her toes.

Seven

The next few days flew by and Gina felt she'd earned every dollar Wade was paying her. She attended meeting after meeting and spent a good deal of time on the boat working on the proposal, double- and triple-checking everything. Wade was tenacious in his approach and meticulous with details. He worked with total concentration. It was only once they were done for the night that he would look at her as if he could devour her.

But they were both drained physically and mentally and Gina was grateful he kept his distance. Three days had gone by since that first episode on the beach where Wade had taken her to the water's edge. And every morning since, he'd persuaded her to take a barefoot stroll along the beach for only a minute or two with him. He'd roll his pants up, remove his shoes and urge her to do the same.

Gina had gotten accustomed to the feel of water lapping over her feet. She'd even gotten used to being below on the yacht, working in Wade's small office or at the navigation station. It was the dinghy rides back and forth to the boat that still frightened her. The small tubular boat that Wade made sure to power slowly to the dock and back, brought her close to the surface of the water and even closer to facing her fears.

And now as she sat in the dinghy, ready to head back to the hotel, Wade made the same request he'd made for the past three days. "Put your hand in the water, Gina."

And Gina gave him the same answer she'd given him for the past three days. "Not today, Wade."

But this time, Wade frowned and shot her a determined look, one she'd readily recognized from days of working alongside him. "We're almost through with our work here. It's now or never."

Gina crossed her arms over her middle. "*Never* sounds good to me."

"Then we may *never* get to shore." Wade steered the dinghy away from the shore, slowly heading the boat out of the bay.

Gina froze. Every muscle in her body tensed. Wade couldn't be serious. He wouldn't do that to her. "Wade, don't."

When he looked at her panicked expression, he

killed the engine and softened his tone. "You've got your life jacket on, we're not in deep water and, Gina, I'm here. I won't let anything happen to you. Trust me."

That wasn't the first time he'd asked for her trust. For anyone else, leaning over to put their hand in the ocean might seem easy as pie, but they hadn't witnessed the water swallowing up their parents.

But Gina also knew it was time to face her fear and not let it dictate her life anymore. On a deeply held breath, Gina, seeking his encouragement fastened her gaze on Wade then leaned over and put her hand in the water. She managed to splash it around, tamping down shivers rising up.

"I'll get back at you for this," she told Wade, without the least bit of sincerity.

"I don't doubt it," he said, with a crooked smile, watching her scoop and sift water around for a few seconds. When she pulled her hand out, he seemed satisfied. And again, he didn't pass it off and remark how easy that was for her. No, she appreciated the fact that Wade knew how hard that simple act was for her.

"Now sit back. We're heading in." He started up the motor again.

And once they docked, Wade helped Gina out of the dinghy, placing a chaste kiss on her lips. "You did good back there."

Gina felt like a child who'd won the spelling bee, a stirring of pride, relief and accomplishment. No one knew the terror she'd felt that day and, finally, with

Wade's help she was learning to accept what happened and overcome her fear. "You gave me no choice."

Wade smiled again. "I know. It's how I operate. But it worked. I think you're slowly coming around. Still want to get back at me?"

Gina looked into his beautiful deep green eyes. "I haven't decided yet."

"You can decide over dinner tonight. No work. Just play. We'll have a quiet meal at the Portofino and celebrate."

"Celebrate?"

"Our work is nearly complete here. The bid is ready and we both deserve some time to relax and enjoy."

Gina closed her eyes, imagining dim lights, soft music and a good meal. "Mmm. That sounds good."

"It will be. Come on, I'll walk you back to the hotel so you can get ready."

When he placed his hand on the small of her back, Gina stopped him. "No. I want to walk along the beach. By myself this time."

Wade looked into her eyes, studying her, then nodded. "Okay. I'll meet you downstairs in the Portofino in three hours."

Gina reached up and kissed Wade on the cheek, remarkably grateful for his heavy-handed tactics. With his help, she was finally regaining the part of herself she'd lost nine years ago.

Wade was early. He'd dressed in a casual light-silk suit and paced the floorboards of *Total Command* wishing the time would move faster. He'd shut off the computer, snapped shut his briefcase with a click and shut down his mind from work. He was ready to play.

With Gina.

He decided he'd be better off waiting at the Portofino having a drink instead of pacing the interior of the boat. So he motored into Avalon and walked the distance to the hotel as the early evening sun set on the horizon.

He was immediately greeted at the restaurant door by Peter, the maître d'. "Good evening, Mr. Beaumont. May I see you to a table?"

"Yes, thank you, Peter. There'll be just two. And I'd like a corner table.'"

"Of course," he said, "right this way."

The maître d' led him to a table in the far corner of the dimly lit room and showed him a seat. "This is fine."

"Are you enjoying your stay here on the island, Mr. Beaumont?"

Wade engaged in light conversation with Peter for the next few minutes. When Peter handed him a wine list, Wade immediately shook his head. "No need. I'll take a whiskey on the rocks. And when the lady arrives, a bottle of your finest champagne."

"Of course. I'll have your drink sent to your table right away."

Once Peter walked away, Wade scanned the restaurant in hope of finding Gina here early as well. No such luck. Then the door opened and Gina strode in, looking stunning in a delicately fitted white halter dress with enough folds and billowy flair to turn every head in the place. She wore her hair down, flowing just past her shoulders in soft waves. Wade rose immediately and took a step forward.

Gina strode directly to the bar and sidled up to a man who had his back to him. Wade stopped his approach, retreated and leaned against the back wall, sipping his drink, watching.

The man bought Gina a drink. They stood talking for a while and then they both turned slightly, so that their profiles were visible.

Blood boiled in Wade's veins the instant he recognized the mysterious man. It was John Wheatley, president and CEO of Creekside Construction, his only real competitor on the island.

What the hell was Gina doing sharing a drink and sweet smiles with him? They seemed deep in thought, with shared whispers and heads close. Obviously, she had no knowledge that he was here. Wade had arrived early on purpose and so had she. She probably didn't suspect he'd be here this early.

A myriad of thoughts ran through Wade's mind, trying to fathom why Gina would be speaking with his competitor.

And then everything became crystal clear.

Wheatley dipped into his jacket and took out a checkbook. He wrote the check, ripped it off and placed it directly into Gina's hand. She didn't bother glancing at the amount; she simply opened her purse and dropped it in. She closed the purse again without hesitation. As though she knew the amount. As though this had all been prearranged.

Wheatley and Gina exchanged a few more words, then he kissed her cheek, giving her one soulful lingering look before exiting.

Wade polished off the remaining whiskey in his glass as Gina's words struck him with full force.

There isn't anything I won't do to clear my name.

I'll do whatever it takes to get out from under all my debt.

Gina had done it again. She'd played him for a fool. To think he'd actually admired her gumption and determination. He'd liked her win-at-any-cost attitude. But he'd been blindsided. He honestly hadn't seen this coming. Yet the woman had practically spelled it out in big bold red letters. She couldn't be trusted. She had a ruthless streak in her that ran down her spineless back.

She'd conspired with the enemy. She had access to all Triple B files, all his ideas and the actual bid on the project. Wade couldn't see past his fury. But he was angrier with himself for letting down his guard. For actually beginning to believe Gina had changed. For nearly falling in love with her again.

She'd shown her true colors tonight. She was a liar and a cheat and Wade planned on making her pay. She wouldn't get away with this. As he slipped out the back door only to enter through the front again, he planned his revenge. He knew exactly what he needed to do.

Gina had put him off far too long.

* * *

Gina finished her chardonnay and was setting the wineglass on the bar just as strong arms wrapped around her waist and pressed her close from behind. Warm breath caressed her throat. "You look gorgeous tonight."

She leaned into him, closing her eyes.

Wade.

His scent alone brought shivers and Gina indulged, drinking in the feel and smell of him, man and musk. Her well-honed defenses were crumbling. She was too happy today to fight it. Things were going well, in all aspects of her life, so why not enjoy the evening with an incredibly appealing man?

"You're early," she said quietly.

Wade turned her in his arms, the flow of her soft white dress brushing his thighs. "I couldn't wait to see you again."

There was intensity on his face and in his green eyes as he cupped her chin and lifted her mouth to his. He kissed her soundly, fully, ending the kiss all too soon. She opened her eyes to find him watching her. "Let's have dinner."

He took her hand and she followed him to a table set for two in the far corner of the restaurant. He seated her and took his own seat. A waiter immediately rushed over with an ice bucket and a bottle of very expensive champagne. He set it down and Wade thanked him before turning to her. "The Portofino is known for outstanding service."

Wade wasted no time pouring from the bottle.

He filled two flutes. Bubbles sparkled to the top as he handed her a tapered glass, his smile warm and charming. "To you, Gina. I've finally come to know the woman you are."

This was a new Wade, one she hadn't seen before. Gina touched her flute to his, pleased with his toast. Had he forgiven her? Had he finally realized that she was a woman to be trusted? Could they really put the past behind them?

Slowly, step by baby step Gina was overcoming her fear of water. She had Wade to thank for that and she was grateful for his dogged persistence. He was a never-say-die kind of man and his relentless efforts had worked. That wouldn't have happened if she hadn't taken this job and come to this island.

The glasses clinked. She stared into Wade's beautiful eyes. "Don't forget Triple B. We should toast to a job well done, Wade."

Wade blinked and she thought she lost him for a moment, but then he smiled and nodded. "Right, Triple B. Let's drink to my company and your role in its success."

Gina lifted her lips to the glass. "It's a team effort."

Wade gazed at her from over the top of the glass then sipped champagne. "And you always like to be on the winning team, right?"

He spoke to her softly, but with intensity in his eyes. Gina knew how important winning this bid was for him. She agreed. "I'm hoping to be."

They finished off the bottle of champagne, dined

on Italian bread, Caesar salad, scampi and a light raspberry mocha tart for dessert as the sound of Sinatra serenaded the softly lit room. By the time the meal ended, Gina's head spun from gourmet food, expensive champagne and Wade's complete and charming attention.

She stood and sighed heavily. "Thank you for the meal. It's been a wonderful night. But I think I'm ready for bed."

Wade was by her side, taking hold of her hand. "I've been thinking that all evening, sweetheart."

Before his comment had a chance to register, Wade wrapped an arm around her waist and guided her out of the dining room, changing the subject as they made their way up to her suite.

He was close. So close. And warm. So warm by her side. Her defenses down, when he took the key-card from her hand to open the door she rested her head on his shoulder as the arm embracing her waist, tightened.

"Th-thank you," she said, "I can manage from here."

Wade shook his head. "I think you need more help," he whispered into her ear, then turned her to face him right before his lips came down on hers. He kissed her long and deep and when he was through, Gina's body quaked with raw emotion.

She didn't know which Wade he really was, the charming sexy man she'd been with tonight or the ruthless, powerful never-say-die man she'd seen this week. It didn't seem to matter. Her heart was melting, along with the rest of her body.

His breath flowed over her lips. "Let me tuck you in."

He folded her into his embrace, meshing their bodies together. His heat became her heat, his desire became her desire. She sighed, realizing she was helpless to stop the flow of passion between them. "I can tuck myself in," she said without a drop of conviction.

Wade reached up to play with the straps of her halter, brushing his fingers along the nape of her neck. "But it's more fun when I do it."

"Is it?" she breathed out.

"Try me."

She had tried him once before and she'd never forgotten. She'd given herself to him wholly and without hesitation and the night had been magical. Later when she believed he'd betrayed her, she'd run far away.

At the time, her friend Sarah didn't know what her lies had cost them. But it was too late for regrets. Maybe now, finally, they could move on.

Wade ushered her into the suite and closed the door behind them, but he didn't let her get far. He grabbed her shoulders with both hands, turned her and crushed her against him, stepping back until the door braced his body. She fell into his embrace, his strong arms circling around her.

A buzzing thrill coursed up and down her body. Her legs went weak. Wade had taken control and this time she gave in to him without resistance. "This is going to happen tonight," he said, his voice a husky whisper.

In the back of Gina's mind, she related him to his yacht, the power and sleek smooth ride that was guaranteed.

Total Command.

"Yes," she sighed, her reply unnecessary as Wade wasted no time. He lifted his hands to the back of her neck and untied the straps of her halter. His gaze left her face to watch the tapered ties loosen then fall to her shoulders. His fingers slid over the material, inching it down, further and further, until the air, warm and sultry, hit her breasts.

Wade looked at them and his breath quickened.

She wanted him to touch her, to put his mouth on her. The look in his eyes was far too tempting.

He struggled out of his jacket, then out of his shirt with Gina frantically helping as they tossed his clothes away.

Wade cupped her from behind, his hands splaying across her cheeks, tugging her closer. She meshed against him, her breasts flattened against his chest, her thighs teased by the strength of his erection.

She felt him. Wanted him. His breaths wafted over her neck, his lips nestled against her throat. He unzipped her dress, then maneuvered it down, catching her white lacy panties along the way until she was buck naked, standing before him in her two-inch heeled sandals.

"Better than I remembered," he rasped out, before spinning her around, so that they'd traded places. Gina's back was now pinned against the door. Her heart hammered hard. Wade gave her no time to think. He was on bended knee before her, stroking her calves, his hands climbing higher now, over her knees to slide smoothly up her thighs.

Sensations roared in her head, her body ached. Her mind shut down. "Open for me, baby," he said, and she did. She spread her legs and his fingers found her core. She jolted when he touched the nub that sparked flaming heat and raw, hot desire. She moaned quietly, the erotic sound reverberating in the stillness of the room.

Wade stroked her for only a second, before his mouth replaced his fingers. Gina cried out, the torturous pleasure, so long in coming, would have buckled her if not for Wade's hold on her waist, firm and unrelenting.

His mouth found her folds and parted them. Then his tongue found it's mark and Gina's temperature soared. He stroked her unmercifully while she moaned and moved, up and down, her body finding a pace and a rotation to meet his fiery demand.

He stood abruptly, grabbed a packet from his trousers before removing the rest of his clothes and in seconds, he was lifting her, fitting her to him. "Lock your legs around me, baby," he commanded, and she did. She watched him watch her, the passion in his eyes a heady elixir.

He entered her slowly, the feel of him inside her only matching the look of pure unmasked undeniable lust on his face. She closed her eyes and threw her head back, taking from him what he offered her. Slowly, as if drawing out the pleasure, he filled her.

And when he moved, she clasped him tight, squeezing out her own pleasure.

She heard him grunt then, a carnal sound of deep gratification and, from then on, he moved with quick powerful thrusts, penetrating her to her depths. He pumped harder, faster almost violently and Gina matched him, fulfilling her deepest yearnings.

He wasn't kissing her or caressing her fondly as he had in the past and Gina recognized a difference in him and the way he made love to her. But her mind and body couldn't quite sort it out. She was beyond that now anyway and she clasped her legs tighter around him, sinking into him, fully immersed in his strength and power.

She knew the exact moment when he towered over the edge. She followed him and panted with each potent deliberate thrust, until both were fully sated and spent.

Wade lowered her until her heels found the floor.

He brought her close and whispered in her ear. "Don't even think about getting dressed. I want you naked and in that bed, all night long."

They were hardly the words of love and adoration she expected. Gina pulled back and away to gaze up at him. For a moment, there was a cold bleak look in his eyes, before he blinked it away. She tried to make sense of it all, but then Wade softened his expression, his eyes turning warm and tender on her right before he kissed her. His lips were gentle and sweet and he cradled her, comforted her, gently caressing her shoulders and then her breasts finally making her feel like a woman who had just been loved.

"You want that, too, don't you, honey?" he asked, a charming smile on his face.

She didn't have to think. She was totally, one-hundred percent in love with Wade Beaumont. She reached up to kiss him soundly on the lips. "There's no place else I'd rather be, Wade."

Wade nodded, then picked her up and carried her to the bed.

The night was just beginning.

Eight

Wade made love to Gina slowly this time, enjoying the full expanse of the king-size bed. Gina relished his hands on her, leisurely seeking, exploring and caressing every part of her body. She lay back against the lush cool sheets, savoring his thorough assault and the kisses that caused a tremor to rumble through her. His mouth knew other tricks as well and she welcomed lips that bestowed pleasure at the base of her throat, her shoulders, her breasts. She offered her body and he took it all without hesitation until she felt as though they were at last truly connected.

Though Wade said little, she felt his desire, the fiery look in his eyes, the heat and passion that he couldn't conceal. She witnessed it all and wished for a future filled with that same lust and craving.

Wade reached up to place her arms above her head. He clasped her hands in one of his and held her there, her fingers scraping the headboard. He thrust into her once, holding firm, absorbing her, his eyes closing. "I wanted this…wanted you since the moment I saw you walk into Aunt Dottie's kitchen."

Opening his eyes to stare into hers, he pumped into her, again slowly. "You were the most beautiful girl I'd ever seen."

"Oh, Wade. I wanted you, too."

But Wade didn't respond to her. He continued. "I wanted a future with you, Gina, but then you ran away."

"Wade," she breathed out softly, "let's not talk about the past. Let's just think about tonight." She didn't want anything to spoil this special time with him.

He stared down into her eyes for a long moment. Then nodded. "Tonight, then," he whispered with a kiss.

Gina sighed happily and hoped this night would finally change their relationship from one of betrayal and doubt to one filled with promise and trust.

She moved her body with his, until the final culmination, collapsing him onto her chest, his breath labored and strong. She held him against her, his powerful body still hot and pulsing. When he rolled onto his back, he took her with him. He wrapped his arms around her and nestled her head under his chin.

She felt safe there and protected and she dozed peacefully for a while, tucked in Wade's strong embrace.

Gina woke up to a cool empty bed. Lazily, she glanced at the digital clock. It was one o'clock in the morning. She lifted up from the bed, searching for Wade. She found him partly dressed, wearing his trousers standing outside with arms braced on the balcony railing, looking out at the sea. A tick in his jaw beat out a rhythm as clear night stars twinkled overhead.

Quietly, Gina rose and threw on Wade's shirt. She tiptoed to the balcony and stood behind him, her heart beating fast. She was so much in love with him that she could barely stand it. But he hadn't spoken of his feelings for her and she knew that for Wade, it would take time. "Can't sleep?"

Wade spun around. The pensive look on his face vanished, but she'd seen it, just for an instant. "I'm just waiting for you."

She pointed to the middle of her chest. "Me?"

His gaze riveted to that place on her chest, then flowed over the rest of her. "I said I wanted you naked all night, but damn. You look hot in that."

A sense of relief swamped her. For a second, she'd seen a look in Wade's eyes that frightened her and threatened this newfound beginning they shared tonight. "Hot?"

He took her into his arms. She relished the feel

of him again, needing his touch. "Sexy, Gina. Gorgeous. You're a man killer, honey."

"Hardly that, Wade." Then she bit down on her lip and tilted her head to ask, "Am I killing you?"

He took her hand and led her back into the suite. "Yeah, I'm a dead man."

Wade plopped onto the bed and coaxed her to straddle him. She crawled over his thighs and looked at him with dewy, half-lidded desire, her heart and body in sync.

He reached for the shirt she wore and lowered it down to bare her shoulders. The shirt pulled open and Wade brought his hands up to rub her erect nipples with his thumbs. A low moan of ecstasy erupted from Gina's throat from the tortured explicit pleasure.

"Kill me again, honey."

Gina pulled his unzipped pants down and off and then fastened the condom before lifting over him, eager to please him, to take him inside her. Once she did, Wade's face tightened, his need and desire fully unmasked now. She moved on him, his erection tight and hard, filling her, fulfilling her and making her complete.

He coaxed her with gentle commands and she rode the waves up and down, his fingers teasing her taut nipples, then his hands lowering to guide her at the waist to set a rapid pace. Passion flowed. She took so much from his eyes, always on her: his desire, need and complete wild abandon.

The ride was crazy hot. Soul-filled and earth-shattering. She climaxed first, shuddering out of control.

"That's it, baby," he rushed out, "give me everything."

And once she did, he rolled her onto her back, taking control and thrusting into her until neither one could move another muscle.

Wade lay back on the bed, breathing hard. "You can bury me, now."

Gina snuggled up close and his arms automatically wound around her. "I'm too tired," she whispered. "Tomorrow."

Wade made a low grunt of a sound. Exhausted, he said quietly, "I don't want to think about tomorrow."

Sunshine made its way through the suite and light rays targeted Wade, hitting his face, waking him from a soundless slumber. Sleep-hazy, he nuzzled Gina's neck, her long flowing hair tickling his throat as they lay together in spoon-like fashion, with his arms wrapped snugly around her. He stroked her soft skin with gentle fingers. The scent of her and of their lovemaking during the night stirred his body once again.

She was the perfect woman for him.

He cupped her breasts, teasing the ripened orbs, then slid one hand along her torso and lower along her thigh. He could go on touching her like this, feeling her smooth sleek perfect skin and he'd never tire of it.

She stirred awake. "Mmm."

Wade nibbled on her throat and with languid movements, Gina turned in his arms. Her beautiful dark-almond eyes opened on him and she sent him a sexy smile. "Morning."

He blinked. And blinked again.

Then he remembered.

The appalling truth struck him like a bludgeoning hammer to his head.

The deceit.

The betrayal.

The check Gina had so willingly taken from his competitor.

I'll do whatever it takes to get out from under all my debt.

Her damning pronouncement slammed into him with rock-hard force. He'd almost forgotten. He'd almost been snared into her trap. He'd shared the best night of his life with a woman he had to write off—a woman who had badly burned him.

For his revenge to be complete, he had to cut her out of his life for good.

Wade winced. He hated her for making him seek revenge, for putting him in this position, for turning his life upside down again.

He'd cut her out, but the knife would slice him up just as badly. He had no choice. He had to protect himself and his company.

He had no use for a woman he couldn't trust.

Wade shoved the covers off abruptly.

Gina's eyes went wide with surprise.

He rose from the bed and looked his fill, drinking in the sight of her lying there, beautifully naked, her inky tresses falling over soft shoulders. Wade knew it would be the last time he'd see her this way.

"Wade?"

Wade pulled his trousers on and zipped them up. "Get dressed," he said harshly.

"Why? Are we late for—"

"Pack your bags. You're fired."

Gina laughed, her eyes dancing with amusement. "What kind of joke is—"

Wade loomed over her, his lips tight, his eyes hard. "It's no joke, Gina. You no longer work for Triple B."

Gina's smile faded fast. She clutched the sheet and covered herself. "You're serious, aren't you?"

Wade grabbed his shirt—the one Gina had tortured him with last night, shoving his arms through the sleeves. Damn, it smelled of her. He didn't bother with buttoning it. "Dead serious."

Gina rose and they faced each other from opposite sides of the bed, her expression not one of guilt but of puzzlement. "I don't understand."

Furious now, thinking about how she'd almost duped him again Wade spoke with deceptive calm. "I saw you last night, Gina. Accepting another bribe. This time from my biggest competitor. Don't deny it, *sweetheart*. You were at the bar last night with John Wheatley. The two of you looked awfully cozy. So don't even try to lie your way out of this one."

But Gina did begin to deny it, by continually shaking her head. "No, no."

"Yes, yes. What kind of woman are you? Hurting me last time wasn't enough?" Thinking of her multiple betrayals only fueled his anger more. "This time you weren't satisfied with destroying my heart. No, that wasn't enough. You set out to destroy my company as well. But you damn well failed. I found out and now I want you out of here."

Gina's face flamed. Her eyes turned black as coal. She took a step toward him, fixing her glare on him. "Are you saying that because you thought I screwed you over, you decided to do the same to me?"

Wade lifted his lips in a smug smile. "I guess the screwing went both ways last night."

"Bastard!"

"Bitch."

Gina closed her eyes as if trying to tamp down her fiery temper. Then she walked over to her purse and dug out the check. "Is this the check you're referring to?"

Out of curiosity, Wade strode over to her to see how much money, was enough for her to sell him out. "Yeah, that's it."

She shoved it up into his face. "Read it, Wade." Then she spoke slowly, and with unyielding determination. "Read it and know that I'll never…ever… forgive you for this."

Wade grabbed the check and looked at it, his mind going numb for a second, as impending dread crept in. "The Survive Foundation?"

Gina snatched the check from his hand and returned it to her purse. Her voice broke with unbridled anger. "When I left El Paso, I thought about ripping up your father's check. Maybe I shouldn't have taken it in the first place, but you see, I thought you had betrayed me. I thought—never mind."

"Tell me, Gina." He softened his voice, realizing that he might have just made a huge mistake, one that would cost him more than this project. "Why would you think I betrayed you?"

Gina immediately backed away from him, as if being near him disgusted her. Her voice elevated. There was fire in her eyes. "That's Sarah's secret to tell, but I will tell you this. I came to Los Angeles, brokenhearted, grieving from the loss of my parents and over losing you. But I had your father's money and I decided to put it to good use. I helped start The Survive Foundation, a nonprofit organization to aid and support survivors of accidents and those who are grieving."

Wade made a move toward her, but she put up her hand and shook her head. "Don't."

It wasn't so much her stance, but the depth of hatred in her eyes, that left him immobile.

She spoke with a rough bitter edge, one Wade had never heard before. "I only know John Wheatley and his wife because they lost a child to leukemia two years ago. The foundation helped them through their loss. I saw them both on the beach yesterday and he wanted to thank me. The check is a donation."

Wade sucked in oxygen as he took this all in.

He'd been wrong about her, misjudging her loyalty and—

"Get out, Wade."

Gina's command startled him. "What?"

"Get out of my room. Get out of my life. I never want to see you again!"

Wade shook his head. "No, I can't leave now. I'll admit that—"

Gina picked up a shoe and threw it at him. He ducked and the sandal missed his head but grazed his shoulder. "Get out!"

"Gina," Wade mustered warning in his tone, though in truth, he'd been poleaxed by her revelations.

"Don't *Gina,* me, Wade. I want you out of this room. Now! I never want to set eyes on you again. You're just like your father…coldhearted and ruthless and I'm tired of your accusations!"

Her voice wobbled and she held back tears. Wade saw the destruction on her face and the hurt. Damn it. Why in hell hadn't she told him all of this before?

Next, she picked up the flower vase from the sofa table, threatening to toss it. "I mean it."

Wade knew her hot temper. And he knew she wouldn't hesitate. He backed out of the room. "I'm going," he said, and exited.

He heard the crash, glass splintering against the door the instant he'd closed it and loud profane curses coming from inside the suite.

He braced his body against the wall, trying to absorb all that had happened already today. He'd been so wrong. And Gina wasn't about to forgive him easily.

Wade winced and massaged his temples. The only thing he could do was give her time to cool off. She wasn't about to speak to him now. And he needed time to sort this all out.

Somehow, he'd make it up to her.

And then he'd talk to Sarah.

Tears streamed down Gina's face, the unbelievable hurt going deep. Wade wasn't worth her tears. She never wanted to see him again. She'd loved him once, and up until this morning had hoped he was still the Wade she'd once known. The man she could trust who'd been caring and kind. But she couldn't love him anymore. And she'd fight it until her last breath not to feel anything for him ever again. He'd shown her his heartless, diabolical, calculating side. She'd been right in accusing him of being just like his father. He was and that spoke volumes for his character.

Gina shoved her clothes into her suitcase. More tears slid down her cheeks. "Bastard, jerk, idiot," she continued on until she couldn't think of any more ways to describe him, while she packed everything up and stormed out, leaving everything Wade had ever given her behind.

She made immediate arrangements with Catalina Express for transportation back to Los Angeles. She was too angry to acknowledge her fear of traveling over the water for ninety minutes on a three-tiered boat, by herself. She'd manage. With suitcase in hand, she ran along Crescent Avenue to the boat landing, rushing to make the earliest departure from the island. Once she handed in her ticket and stepped aboard, she felt not fear, but an uncanny sense of relief to be completely rid of Wade Beaumont and this island.

She braced herself, holding onto the railing. Once a few more passengers boarded, the boat motored up and took off. Gina faced her fear, forcing herself to look out over the ocean. She had more than an hour to endure on the Pacific and, once she reached the San Pedro dock, she'd have to face her future as well as her fears. One that did not include Wade Beaumont or Triple B.

And though the trip had been a test of her will, keeping herself composed while the Express glided over waves and headed home was far easier than for-getting the hurtful image of Wade as he loomed over the bed they'd just made love in. He'd coldly dis-missed and fired her, demanding that she pack her bags.

He hadn't even given her the benefit of the doubt.

Or asked her up front about John Wheatley and the check she'd been given.

He'd deliberately seduced her, not out of love or compassion, but for revenge—to teach her a lesson.

And he'd gotten his revenge—a job well done. Gina had made it easy for him. She'd laid it all out on the line for him and he'd crushed her in one sweeping blow.

But just a few hours later, as Gina sat on her tiny sofa, opening the week's mail, her hand shook at the wedding invitation staring back at her. Another blow, this one not as shocking. But the timing and irony was almost too much to bear.

> **Mr. and Mrs. Charles Buckley request the honour of your presence**
> **at the marriage of their daughter**
> **Sarah Nicole Buckley**
> **To**
> **Roy Zachary Winston**

The rest of the words blurred as Gina's eyes misted up. After nine years, Sarah had finally gotten the man of her dreams. She'd hung in there and worked it all out.

If only Sarah hadn't told those lies nine years ago.

Then maybe Gina's whole life might have turned out differently and she, too, would have gotten the man of her dreams.

Too bad that man didn't exist anymore.

Nine

Wade slammed the phone down for the tenth time in three days. He glanced at the work piling up on his desk, the contracts he needed to go over, the payroll checks he needed to sign, but he couldn't concentrate on any of it.

Gina refused his calls. She wouldn't pick up. He got her answering machine each and every time. "Damn you, Gina."

He lifted the wedding invitation on his desk, staring at it with unblinking eyes. And the note attached. Sarah had been trying to reach him all week.

They'd finally spoken.

Wade spun around in his leather swivel chair and

stared out the big bay window. Summer gloom had set in, but even through the afternoon haze he could see the ocean, blue waters now appearing gray and dingy from the low-lying cloud cover.

Gina had crossed that Pacific. Without him. She'd faced her fears alone. He'd driven her to that. And now she refused to speak with him.

He recalled his surprise when he went back to the Villa Portofino just hours later, ready with a dozen red roses, a heartfelt apology and willing to do whatever it took to make it up to her, only to find her gone.

The hotel clerk refused to divulge any information. Wade used his influence and status, calling over the manager to extract the information. That's when he found out she'd checked out and booked a ticket on the next boat back to the mainland.

Wade hadn't seen it coming. He'd been shocked. He knew she'd been furious with him, but to actually take it upon herself to leave the island alone and fight her fear of the water, told him one very key thing—getting her back wasn't going to be easy.

"To hell with it," he muttered, standing up and jamming his hands in his jacket sleeves. He fished through the papers on his desk, until he came up with what he was looking for. Shoving the envelope in his inside pocket, he strode to the door.

One way or another, Gina was going to speak to him.

And it was going to happen tonight.

* * *

Gina brought her dinner dish to the kitchen sink and thanked her landlord and friend, Delia, once again. "The meal was delicious, Dee. Thank you. I needed this."

"I know you did. And I'm glad you finally agreed to our invitation. Marcus and I have been worried about you."

Gina tightened the elastic band on her ponytail and shrugged with a heavy sigh. Her landlords had been such wonderful moral support lately. Once she'd returned from Catalina, they'd spotted her sullen demeanor immediately and tried to cheer her up with home-baked cookies, hand delivered mango margaritas and invitations to dine out with them. She hadn't been in the mood for any of it. But, finally, tonight she'd accepted their dinner invitation and told them the whole story, from El Paso to Catalina and everything in between. "I'll be fine…soon."

Delia took the plates and rinsed them then handed them one at a time to Gina, who was arranging them in the dishwasher.

"You know, it's okay for you not to be…fine. I mean, don't knock yourself out convincing yourself everything is wonderful when it's not. Allow yourself time."

Gina wiped her damp hands on her jeans. She'd been slumming it lately, dressing down and laying low while searching the classifieds for the past few days. The job hunt was not going well. Gina's heart wasn't in it. "Time for what?"

Delia only smiled, her eyes insightful. "Just time, honey."

Gina wished she had the luxury of time. But she needed to move on with her life and the sooner the better.

"Oh and don't you worry about the rent this month. Marcus and I don't want you stressing about it."

"I have rent money, Dee. I'm not broke." Her heart had broken, but fortunately her tiny bank account hadn't, not just yet.

"No, but you have that wedding this month, don't you? It'd do you good to see the Buckleys again. Don't you think so?"

Gina had forgiven Sarah for her unwitting crimes years ago and she was happy for her, but attending anyone's wedding right now was the last thing she wanted to do. Yet she wanted to be there for Sarah and the Buckleys. "Yes, they've always been kind to me. I wouldn't miss seeing them. Sarah and I, well, we've had some drama in our lives, but we're still good friends. She's asked me to be in the wedding party."

"The change of scenery will do you good."

Marcus popped his head in the kitchen doorway. "Care for coffee outside, ladies? Stars are out to-night."

"That sounds nice, sweetheart," Dee said to him, then turned to Gina. "Coffee?"

Gina smiled and shook her head. "No thanks. Not tonight."

Marcus strode into the room to place his arm

around her shoulder. "I can't coax you into decaf? It won't keep you awake, I promise."

Gina chuckled. She wished caffeine were all that was keeping her from sleep these past few nights. "I really should be going. I'd like to do some reading."

Marcus squeezed her shoulders tight. "You hang in there, Gina." He kissed her forehead and Dee gave her a big hug.

"I'll bring over that book I was telling you about," Dee said, slanting her husband a look. "Marcus misplaced it, but I know it's somewhere in the house. I'll look for it again."

"Thanks, I'd like that. Dinner was great."

"We'll do it again soon."

"Ciao, my friends," Gina said to both of them as she walked out the back door and across the lawn to her humble but homey little guesthouse.

Once inside, she settled in, propping her feet up on the sofa with a glass of iced water and a handed down copy of *Vogue*. She glanced at her answering machine, relieved to see no new messages. She'd hoped Wade had given up calling her. Having her nerves go raw each time the phone rang was an added strain she could do without.

Gina opened the magazine and glanced at the pages. She liked to keep up on fashion, comparing the newest creations on the shelves to those in her head and finding that she always liked hers better.

One day, she'd have her own company. She hadn't given up on that dream.

When the knock came, Gina bounced up and opened the door wearing a smile. "Dee, you found the book already!"

But it wasn't Dee standing there holding a copy of *The Devil Wears Prada*. No, it was another *devil* entirely, one with bold green eyes and a solid steadfast stance. Her first thought was that she'd missed him. But she killed that thought instantly, her second thought being that she hated him. Still.

And her third thought was that he looked so darn handsome, standing there, wearing tailored Armani and a sincere expression that he took her breath away. "Whatever book you need, I'll get it for you."

"What I *need* is for you to leave," she managed quite elegantly and began to close the door.

Wade's arm jutted out, preventing that from happening. His expression fierce now, his eyes raging, he said. "We need to talk. Now. I'm tired of you refusing my calls."

Gina played innocent, just to annoy him. "Oh? Did you call? I don't recollect."

He pushed the door wide open and moved past her, letting himself in. Gina looked out at Marcus and Delia having coffee across the lawn in the patio. Marcus immediately stood, his gaze pensive as he was about to approach. Gina shook her head and gestured that all was okay.

She had to deal with Wade sometime. She knew he wasn't the kind of man to let things drop. No, he always had to have the last word.

"No more games, Gina."

"Spoken from the expert," she blurted as she took her seat on the sofa and opened the magazine again, flipping through pages she really didn't see.

He looked around. "This is nice."

"Hardly a beachside resort," she answered casually.

Wade sat down next to her and took the magazine from her hand. He set it down on the small table next to the sofa. "You're forgetting I came from humble beginnings, too."

Gina rubbed her hands up and down her jeans and then fidgeted with her ponytail. She knew her appearance wouldn't win awards, yet the look in his eyes told her it didn't matter. He caressed her with that look and made her nervous. "What do you want, Wade?"

He smiled and stared at her for a long moment. "I know the truth. I spoke with Sarah."

"And?"

Wade leaned back against the sofa cushion, making himself comfortable. "And I'm pissed. Royally pissed."

"That makes two of us." Gina sent him a wry smile.

Wade shook his head. "I had no idea. All this time, I had no idea that Sarah used me as a shield for Roy Winston."

"She was in love with Roy and she knew her parents would go ballistic if they found out. They'd warned her not to get involved with Roy. He was bad news."

Wade agreed. "He *was* bad news. He'd been suspended from high school, what, three or four times. His parents were the town drunks."

"After college, when we came back to El Paso, I remember the Buckleys telling Sarah that nothing had changed with the Winstons and Roy had gotten arrested for a barroom brawl."

Wade nodded solemnly, "Yeah, I remember that. I was there. Roy got a bad rap. Five of us were there, but the sheriff chose to arrest only Roy. He was known as a troublemaker in town, so naturally they blamed him, but all of us were just as guilty."

Gina went on, "So when Sarah thought she was pregnant, she panicked. She loved Roy, but knew her parents would never accept him. Mr. Buckley had just been diagnosed with a heart condition. Sarah feared it would send her father over the edge. She named you as the father of her baby. She knew her parents liked you, at least. They would accept it. But she didn't know that we had gotten close. If you remember, Sarah had been gone that week with her mother. I never had the chance to tell Sarah my feelings for you.

"She was only trying to protect her family. And Roy. When she told me you had fathered her baby, I was in shock. We'd just been together and I thought…"

Wade pursed his lips and leaned forward, bracing his elbows on his knees. "You thought the worst of me. The very worst."

Gina bounded up abruptly and lashed out. "What

else could I think? My best friend confided in me that you, the man I'd fallen in lo—the man I'd just had sex with for the very first time in my life, was going to be her baby's father."

"Sit down, Gina. And calm down."

"No! You don't know the hell I went through. I was so lost…so vulnerable. I couldn't tell my best friend. I'd begun to hate you and then your father showed up with the bribe. It was a way out. I couldn't stick around El Paso anymore. Not thinking you and Sarah were going to have a child together. So I took the money."

"I hated you for that."

"I know. I wanted you to. It was the only way I could think of to make sure you stayed in El Paso with Sarah. But I used your father's money for a good cause. I'm not sorry I took it. But I am sorry about the circumstances."

"And the irony of all this is that Sarah is marrying Roy," Wade said.

Gina took in a breath, amazed at how things had worked out. "He left El Paso right after that barroom brawl incident and turned his life around. He's successful now, owns his own body shop and is doing well. He came back for Sarah. He'd always loved her."

Wade stood and paced the confines of her room. "Sarah was never pregnant."

"No, she wasn't. It was a false alarm, but I only found that out later on. I'd lost contact with her. Deliberately. But she tracked me down and told me the truth a few years later. And I told her the truth about us. She was mortified, so sorry about all of it. She'd been so wrapped up with hiding her secret about Roy that she hadn't a clue about how we felt about each other. She wanted to find you and tell you the truth too, but I stopped her. What good would it do? By then, you were working in Houston with your father and I was involved with—"

"Another man."

"Yes. That's right." Gina hoisted her chin. "I'd moved on."

"So did I. But I never forgot you."

Gina let out a rueful nervous chuckle. "Right, plotting a way to hurt me. Well, it worked. Congratulations. You got your revenge, didn't you, Wade?"

Wade's voice elevated slightly, "I thought you were out to ruin my company."

Gina faced him now, coming to stand toe to toe with him. She looked at his face and condemned him with the truth. "You used me, used my body. You took something precious and made it ugly. How little you must think of me to believe that I'd sleep with you right after accepting a bribe to ruin you and your company. I don't know why you're here, but I'd like you to leave." She strode past him to open the front door. "There's nothing more to say."

Wade's green eyes flashed with indignation. She'd angered him and she was glad. It was about time someone put Wade Beaumont in his place.

Wade stood still for a moment, staring at her, then removed an envelope from his coat pocket. He set it down on the table. "We won the bid on the Catalina project. Your bonus is in there, along with your paycheck."

Gina nodded, glancing at the envelope, but said nothing. She'd earned that money—the hard way.

Wade strode to the door quickly and stopped to look deeply into her eyes. "You should have told me the truth, right from the beginning."

With that, Wade walked straight out of her life, without so much as a glance back.

Wade stared out as night fell on the Pacific Ocean. He leaned against his deck railing watching the tide creep in then recede back into the darkness of the sea. Only a few stars illuminated the sky, the night as black as his mood.

"You haven't touched your champagne, little brother," Sam said, coming up to stand beside him. He sipped from his glass and leaned against the railing. "Or would you rather have a cold beer?"

Wade shook his head. "No."

"I flew all the way out here from Texas to help you celebrate. Hell, it isn't every day a company wins the biggest bid in its history. You did it, Wade. You should be proud. Instead, I find you here looking like death warmed over."

Wade let out a self-deprecating laugh. "That's one way to describe me. Others might say you're being too kind."

"Others? Or only one other, as in Gina Grady?

"That's the only *other* that matters," Wade admitted.

"Ah," Sam said, sipping his Dom Pérignon. "So how is my old friend?"

"Intelligent, sweet, dedicated and gorgeous."

"Sounds like the Gina I remember."

Wade finally succumbed. He gulped his drink, emptying the glass in five seconds flat. "She's not a fan."

Sam chuckled. "So she's got more brains than most women. She didn't throw herself at your feet?"

Wade muttered a curse, directing it right at Sam.

He chuckled again. "Kidding. Hey, what's really up? I come here expecting a party, and you look like—"

"Death warmed over?" Wade finished for him.

"I was about to say, like you lost your best friend."

Wade grabbed the bottle and poured another drink. "Maybe I did. I made some mistakes with Gina. Now she doesn't want to have anything to do with me."

Sam's smile faded. "You're serious about her?"

Wade nodded.

Sam reflected, this time on a serious note. "I thought you two were a perfect match, even back in El Paso. That's why I recommended her for the job here in L.A., little brother. I thought, you two would pick up where you left off. I take it there's problems?"

"You don't want to know," Wade said, sipping his drink again, this time slowly and savoring the taste, letting it glide down his throat.

"I do want to know. I'm here. Lay it on me."

Wade turned to Sam. "It's a long story."

Sam smiled and put his hand on Wade's shoulder. "I'm not going anywhere."

They sat in the deck chairs for the next thirty minutes, polishing off the Dom, while Wade explained to Sam his situation, leaving out some of the more intimate details.

And after hearing him out, Sam leaned back in his chair, staring up at the stars. "Well, the easiest thing to do is forget her. Move on. Concentrate on the project."

He eyed Wade then, with an arched brow.

Wade scoffed, "Not possible. She's hard to forget. If I couldn't do it in nine years, I certainly can't do it now."

Sam smiled. "Okay, that was the first test. You passed, by the way."

Wade didn't smile back. "So I get an *A*. Any other bright ideas?"

Sam leaned in, and spoke directly at him, in all seriousness. "You going to Sarah's wedding?"

Wade inhaled sharply. "I haven't decided yet."

"Can't forgive her?"

"Hell, she wants me to be in the wedding party. She apologized up, down and sideways. I can't really blame her. I understand about Roy. What happened, well, it happened. It was nine years ago. I told her I'd think about it."

"If I were you, I wouldn't think too long. Gina's going and she's in the wedding."

"How do you know that?"

"Because Caroline called Sarah to say we can't go to the wedding and Sarah told her all about the wedding plans. We promised to visit soon; it would be good to see Uncle Lee and Aunt Dottie again. Besides, we have news of our own."

Wade's head snapped up. "What news?"

Sam's mouth stretched into a big grin. "We're going to have a baby. Caroline's pregnant."

Wade bounded up from his seat and Sam rose, too. He hugged his brother and myriad emotions streamed in. Happiness for his brother and the second chance he'd gotten with Caroline and her little daughter Annabelle, but then a shot of envy filtered in as well. For the first time in his life, Wade wanted what Sam had. A wife and family. And he wanted Gina to fill that role. "Geez, why didn't you say so sooner?"

Sam laughed. "She'll be pregnant eight more months. There's no rush. I wanted to tell you in person. And we're going to visit her folks in Florida to tell them the news firsthand, too. That's why we can't make Sarah's wedding."

Then Sam took his shoulder, his smile fading some. "Remember when you came out to Hope Wells and saw me with Caroline at her stables? Then later, when I left her, unable to face losing my own child, you made me see that I had a second chance in life. You made me take that chance. And now, not only did I adopt little Annabelle, I'm going to be a father again. I've got a wonderful wife and family and this time I'm doing it right. We all make mistakes, Wade. Go after what you want."

Wade hesitated, scrubbing his jaw. "I've already had a second chance with Gina. Seems the stars aren't aligned with the two of us. She's accused me of being like our father—ruthless, cold, hardhearted. And you know, I'm beginning to believe it myself."

"That's crap, little brother. You're not your father's son. You never have been."

"She walked out on me so easily the first time. Seems that the people I care about most, don't give a sh—"

"Gina does. I guarantee it. She cares for you. From what you said, she didn't so much run away from you as the situation. Okay, so you blew it the second time. Call it even. Take another chance. The third time's the charm, they say. Go to that wedding. Make her see the real you and not some replica of Blake Beaumont."

Wade scratched his chin, pondering.

Sam prodded, "If you don't, you'll regret it the rest of your life."

Wade knew that Sam was right. He had to go to that wedding. He'd never been one to back down from a challenge. And Gina posed the biggest challenge of his life. He'd falsely accused her and hurt her deeply. Turning her feelings around would take nothing short of a miracle. "She can't stand the sight of me."

Sam chuckled, seemingly sure that Wade could pull this off. "That's the best way to start. You can only improve from there."

Wade had to smile at his brother's optimism. "I'll call Sarah. Let her know I'll be coming to her wedding after all."

Ten

Gina packed her bags, telling herself she needed this time away. Sarah had been thrilled that she'd accepted not only the invitation, but a place by her side up at the altar as a bridesmaid. She'd put this wedding together in a matter of weeks, wanting to marry Roy as soon as possible. She'd wasted enough of her life and she was ready to finally begin her future with the man she loved. Gina understood that all too well.

She'd wasted time on Wade, but her future was destined to play out much differently.

On a sigh, she snapped close her suitcase, took one look around, making sure she hadn't forgotten anything, then picked up her traveling case. She slung it over her shoulder and wheeled her luggage to the front door.

Sarah had her bridesmaid dress waiting for her in El Paso and had coaxed her into coming a week early to be a part of the pre-wedding arrangements, seeing to the decorations, favors, music and of course, to attend the rehearsal and dinner afterward.

Sarah's happiness was contagious and Gina couldn't say no. Besides, Sarah insisted that her dress would need an alteration or two. How could she argue with that? So she locked up her house and walked outside to meet Delia who had quite generously offered to take her to the airport.

When she got halfway down the long drive, Delia stepped into view, her usual jovial face, looking tentative.

"Hi, Dee. Anything wrong?"

Dee took the handle of Gina's luggage and began walking along the path towards the front of the house. "I hope not, honey.

"I hope not, too. What's up?" Gina asked, her curiosity escalating. Dee was the most laid-back, honest person she knew. Usually, she didn't skirt around issues or appear apprehensive. Right now, she was doing both.

"I hope I made the right decision."

Again, Gina hadn't a clue what she meant.

Dee opened the large swinging gates beside the front of the house that led to the street and both walked out.

Then Gina stopped.

And couldn't believe her eyes.

Wade stood at attention beside a stretch limousine, wearing jeans and boots and enough cowboy charm to set her heart racing.

She turned to Dee. "What is he doing here?"

"Apparently, taking you to El Paso."

"What?" Gina's temper flared. She glanced at Wade, who was about to approach when Dee halted him with a stopping hand.

Dee halted him with a stopping hand?

"What's going on, Dee?"

"He called about a week ago. We met him for dinner and he explained what he wanted to do."

"We? You and Marcus? He's got you on his side now?"

Dee shook her head. "No, we're on your side. We always have been. But he's sincere. And he cares for you. Marcus and I, we talked about this and think this is the right thing to do. You two need time to talk, to clear the air. You both need another chance. He wants to take you to El Paso."

Gina's eyes nearly bugged out. "He's kidnapping me?"

Dee grinned. "Romantic, isn't it?"

This time Gina rolled her eyes.

Dee turned so that her back was to Wade who stood twenty feet away. She spoke softly, "He's in love with you, honey."

Gina didn't believe it for one second. No one could convince her of that. "He didn't say that to you."

"No. He didn't have to."

Gina glanced at Wade who was wearing dark sunglasses. She couldn't make out his expression.

"God, Dee. He could have just asked me. See, this is what I mean about him. He's so calculating. He even got you involved in this."

"Gina," Dee began with all seriousness, "any guy who would go to this much trouble for you can't be all bad. He talked to us for hours and we both came away knowing that this guy really cares about you. And besides, we both know that if he had asked you, you would have turned him down flat."

"That's right. He could have respected my wishes. Well, I'm not going to El Paso with him."

"I'm afraid you are," the deep voice resonated from just behind Dee. Both women looked up at Wade. He wasn't smiling. "We both have to get there today. We might as well travel together."

Gina shot back. "I have my own ticket, thank you very much."

"Do you?" he asked, turning to look at Dee.

Dee appeared as though she wanted to slink into the sidewalk. "Honestly, Gina, I didn't think you'd fight this so hard. I thought you wouldn't mind if I cancelled the reservation I made for you."

"What?" Gina couldn't believe this. Dee, the traitor, had fully succumbed to Wade's charm. He could pour it on when he had to. "You cancelled my reservation?"

"Sorry," she said, "but I wanted to save you the money."

Wade took hold of her luggage handle and grabbed

the traveling bag from Gina's shoulder. She'd been too floored to stop him. "I've got a chartered plane waiting for us. I'd like you come with me, Gina."

"Why, Wade? Why do you want me to come with you?"

Wade removed his sunglasses and peered into her eyes. "I miss you."

It was such a clear, honest, simple statement that she couldn't quite stop her heart from accelerating. She'd missed him, too, the Wade she'd fallen in love with. She glanced at Dee, who smiled with hope in her eyes. Gina felt somewhat defeated. She could fold her arms across her middle and declare that she wasn't going. But that would seem childish. And even though she fumed at Wade's tactics, she couldn't deny that he *had* gone to some trouble for her. Riding to the airport in a limousine and flying on a chartered plane to El Paso might not be so bad after all. Besides, his latest admission nearly knocked her to her knees.

He missed her.

"I have a fitting at three o'clock at the bridal salon, so we might as well get going."

Dee smiled in relief.

For a second Wade's mouth crooked up before he took her luggage and handed it to a chauffeur who seemed to have appeared out of nowhere.

The same way Wade had.

Gina tried to relax in the plush leather seat on the Falcon 50, Wade's chartered plane. She had to admit that traveling this way sure beat the lines, the crowds and the coach seat that had been waiting for her at LAX.

Wade sat in the seat facing her, a small polished teak table between them set with a vase filled with white lilies.

Classy.

Gina glanced out the window, peering down at the tiny dotting of houses below, fully aware that Wade's eyes were on her. She felt his perusal and it heated her and made her think of the night they'd spent together in Catalina. She wondered if he was thinking the same thing.

Finally, she faced him. "You're staring at me."

Wade smiled. "I like what I see."

His voice mellow, his eyes warm on her, Gina couldn't help but be affected. "I wish you wouldn't."

Wade leaned way back in his seat. "Why?"

He was making her uncomfortable but she wouldn't admit it. "Don't you have something to do?"

"We could eat something. Coffee? Or breakfast? What would you like?"

Gina's stomach was in knots. "I couldn't eat a thing. Thank you."

He nodded and watched her. She blinked and blinked again, only to see him smiling again.

She'd been with him for six days on that island and she hadn't seen the man crack more than an occasional grudging smile, yet here he was looking at her, smiling like a schoolboy just given an *A* on his report card.

"Do I make you nervous, Gina?"

Oh, yes. "No. Of course not."

He nodded again. "Want to talk?"

She shook her head. "Not particularly."

He nodded once again and continued staring at her.

"There must be something you could do," she said, keeping the irritation out of her voice.

"Yeah, work. But that wouldn't be polite, would it?"

But staring at her with those gorgeous green eyes *was* polite? "Oh, I wouldn't mind. Go right ahead, Wade. Really, you must have a ton of work to do, now that you've won the Catalina project."

Wade reached over the seat and brought his briefcase into view. He set it down on the seat next to him and pulled out a stack of papers. "I'd rather look at you," he muttered.

Inwardly, Gina smiled, but she reminded herself not to fall victim to his charm. "You'd get further with those papers."

He glanced up. "That so?"

She didn't hesitate. "Yes."

Wade's eyes flickered, but he seemed to hold back a comment then he spread the papers out, sorting through them. "You know, you and I made a good team. Technically, you're still on the payroll. I could use help here."

Gina clamped her mouth shut, to keep it from falling open. She was still on the payroll? "You fired me, remember?"

Wade stopped sorting through the paperwork, to look deep into her eyes. "That was a mistake."

"Doesn't matter. I would have quit, anyway," she shot back quickly.

"But you didn't quit and your next check is in the mail."

Surprised, Gina's nerves teetered on end. She'd thought she was through with Triple B for good. But apparently Wade had had second thoughts. She glanced at the Catalina papers—projections, finance reports, estimates—and admitted, for what it was worth, that she had enjoyed the work. "You mean you don't think I'd try to foil your project, in some dastardly way?"

Wade cast her a look of disgust. "No, I know you wouldn't. Can you give me a break?"

"Why, did you give me one?" Oh, that came out more harshly than she intended, but the sentiment remained.

"No. I didn't. But you wanted me to believe the worst about you the first time."

"And the second time? In Catalina?"

"That was a mistake on my part. And I apologize."

Humbled now, Gina realized she had never heard Wade Beaumont apologize for anything, to anyone. "Still, I can't work with you. You don't trust me."

"Yes I do. I'd trust you with my life."

The sincerity of his words filled her head and warmed her heart. But how could she learn to trust him again?

Instead of dealing with it, she grabbed a stack of papers and bent her head, looking them over. "What do you need me to do?"

* * *

When the plane landed at El Paso International Airport, Wade escorted her off, carrying their luggage. A taxi stood waiting for them and soon Gina was back on the streets of El Paso as all sorts of memories rushed in.

"Have you ever been back?" Wade asked.

She shook her head. "No. Sarah and I have met a few times over the years, but always on the West Coast. I haven't seen Chuck and Kay Buckley since I left nine years ago."

Wade sighed. "I'd only seen them a few times, myself. Now, I understand why they'd been distant to me those times I did see them. But Sarah has owned up to the truth to everyone now. Her conscience is clear."

"And what about your aunt and uncle? Do you see them?"

"I would like to see them more. Starting up the company on the West Coast prevented that. But I've gone back for a few quick holidays trips and I've flown them out a few times to visit me."

Gina gazed through the window as they headed out of town and the city landscape rolled into a more rural one. Large fallow fields came into view alongside the fields that grew Egyptian cotton. Roadside poppies dotted the highway and, off in the distance, Gina noted the reddish hilltops of Franklin Mountain where she'd gone hiking with Wade, Sarah and Sam once. Fifteen minutes later, the cab pulled up to the Buckleys' small ranch house.

"Looks like they've painted the house, but everything else seems pretty much as I remembered."

"Things don't change much in small towns," Wade said, helping her out of the taxi and grabbing her luggage.

"Oh, I'll get that," she said, but before she had a chance to retrieve her things, Sarah raced down the steps, her shoulder-length blond hair bouncing as she approached with a big smile.

"Oh, you two came together," she said, hugging Gina immediately, "that makes me happy."

Sarah turned to Wade, her smile more tentative and a look of complete remorse on her face. "I'm forgiven, right?"

Wade looked at Sarah for a moment and Gina's heart ached for her. Gina knew firsthand his heartless wrath and she hoped for Sarah's sake Wade still considered her a friend. She didn't want Sarah's joy being marred one tiny bit, not when she'd finally made peace with everyone and was marrying the man she'd always loved.

When Wade put out his arms, Sarah climbed in and the two hugged for a long moment. "I wouldn't have agreed to be in your wedding otherwise."

Sarah pulled back and looked at both of them. "Thank you for your forgiveness and for agreeing to be in my wedding. It means a lot to me. And to Roy. You'll have to get to know him again, Wade. He's great."

"Obviously he is if you're marrying him."

Sarah's blue eyes lit. "I can hardly believe it after all this time."

"It's always been Roy, and you were smart enough to realize it," Gina said.

"Thanks." Sarah squeezed Gina's hand. "I'm so glad you're here. Mom and Dad can't wait to see you again."

"How are your parents?" Gina asked.

"They're fine. They've finally come around and have accepted Roy. Come inside, both of you."

Wade shook his head. "I'm anxious to see Uncle Lee and Aunt Dottie, but I'll come by tonight after supper. Besides, I hear you're all going to the bridal salon soon."

Sarah darted a quick glance at Gina. "That's right. We have a fitting in a few hours! Oh, this is wonderful having you both here."

Wade took Gina's suitcases to the front door. "I'll see you later," he said then strode past them, toward the taxi. Before getting inside, he stopped and looked at Gina. "I'm glad you decided to join me on the trip."

Gina nodded, biting her lip, and Sarah waved farewell but as soon as the taxi drove off, Gina muttered, "You didn't really give me a choice."

Sarah looked at her then laced an arm through hers as they walked to the front door. "Gina, you are definitely going to have to fill me in on what's really happening with the two of you. As soon as you say hello to my folks, you're spilling the beans."

Gina had to smile.

She didn't know why exactly, but it felt good to be back in El Paso.

"I've missed your pot roast, Aunt Dottie," Wade said, filling his plate a second time. "No one makes it better."

"It's your favorite," she said, passing him the mashed potatoes. He scooped another clump onto his plate and dug in. "I didn't forget."

Wade finished his next bite. "You're still set on fattening me up."

She laughed, the simple, sweet sound, reminding him of good times sitting around this table, with Sam by his side. Aunt Dottie always had a smile and a kind word.

Uncle Lee tapped his flat belly. "See this? The woman's put me on a diet. I only get pot roast when you or Sam come to visit."

"You look great," Wade said, looking over at his father's brother and seeing no resemblance. Uncle Lee had a kindly face and a loyal nature. He loved his wife, his home and his family above all else. "Aunt Dottie takes good care of you, so no complaining."

"You tell him, Wade," his aunt jested.

"I'm not complaining," he said grudgingly, looking over at Wade's plate of food, "but I wouldn't mind a second helping myself."

"Go on, Lee," Dottie said, "I'm not stopping you."

Uncle Lee reached over and forked another piece of pot roast onto his plate. "There's nothing better than the love of a good woman."

Lee winked at his wife and Dottie grinned before setting her gaze on Wade. "Speaking of a good woman, you said that you brought Gina with you. How is that girl?"

Uncle Lee chimed in, "Still pretty as sunshine? Giving you heart palpitations?"

Wade chuckled, then sipped his iced tea. "She's fine. Gorgeous as ever and won't have a thing to do with me."

Aunt Dottie put her hand over his in a consoling manner. "Now, dear. Don't let that stop you. Weddings have a way with people and she might just come around while she's here."

Wade finished his meal, tossed his napkin and pulled back from his chair. "I'm not only banking on that, I'm going to make it happen."

"So Gina's the one?" she asked, darting a quick glance at her husband.

Wade nodded while taking his plate to the sink. "Now it's time to convince her of that. Mind if I saddle up Rio? I'm going over to the Buckleys tonight."

"Not at all, that boy needs the exercise. And say hello to Kay and Chuck for us," his uncle said.

"Will do." Wade bent to kiss his aunt's cheek. "Thanks for supper."

Uncle Lee smiled up at him. "It's good to have you home, son."

Wade no longer flinched when his uncle called him "son." For years, he resented it, but as he grew older, he realized that it felt natural. He wasn't his father's son, but Lee Beaumont's son and he was out to prove that to Gina and the rest of the world if he had to.

Fifteen minutes later, after greeting the Buckleys, Wade stood in their modest living room with Stetson in hand, completely captivated by Gina from the moment she entered the room wearing a pale-pink flowing bridesmaid dress. Her face bright, her deep-brown eyes dancing, she twirled around, unaware that he watched her.

"See, the dress only needed a tiny alteration," Sarah said. "I won't say where, but Gina's bustier than the rest of us girls!"

"Sarah!" Gina playfully admonished her friend but her smile remained.

Wade's gaze riveted to that particular part of her anatomy and memories washed over him, of touching her there, putting his lips to her breasts and tasting her, loving her and making their world spin out of control.

When finally, he looked up she met his eyes…and knew what he'd been thinking.

"You look pretty, Gina," he said.

She took a swallow. "Thank you."

The mood was broken when Roy Winston entered the house and everyone was re-introduced. Wade had to admit that Roy had changed. He, too, had been a product of his parents' discord while growing up, but he'd worked himself out of that fathomless hole and came back to El Paso a new man, one who knew what he wanted. Wade had never seen Sarah or Roy so happy.

Gina went into the bedroom to change out of her dress, while the rest of the group retired to the back porch. She returned wearing blue jean shorts and a red-and-white polka-dotted midriff-exposing blouse, looking every bit an exotic version of Daisy Duke. As the evening pressed on, Wade couldn't help glancing at her every chance he got and when the evening was about to end, he took his shot, blocking the doorway as she started to head inside the house.

"It's a nice night. Take a walk with me."

She began shaking her head. "That's not a good idea."

"Come on, Gina. I'll have you back here in twenty minutes."

"I'm a little tired, Wade. It's been a long day. And tomorrow I'm spending the day working on wedding favors with Sarah and her mother."

"All the more reason to take a walk with me. I won't be seeing you tomorrow."

Gina sighed. "Wade."

"I've got something to show you."

"I bet you do," she rushed out, with a hint of playful teasing in her tone. Wade was encouraged.

"We can take Rio, if you're not up to walking."

"*Rio?*" Gina's face lit at the mention of the gelding's name. He'd once been her favorite. "I'm glad to hear he's still around."

"He isn't as feisty as he once was, but he's healthy. Come on, Gina. What do you say?"

Gina debated for several seconds, keeping him waiting. Wade wasn't a patient man, but he was learning and Gina was worth the time. "I want to be in bed in twenty minutes."

Wade stifled a witty reply. Nothing would make him happier, but he knew Gina wasn't including him in her bedtime plans.

He took her hand. "Let's go."

Eleven

"Tell me about your designs," Wade said, as they walked along a path leading to the Beaumont ranch, Rio clip-clopping along beside them.

"They're unique." Gina never minded speaking about her passion. She still had her old designs in her head and loved thinking up new ones. She had begun a new file, recreating the designs she'd lost and adding sketches of the new ones she created. "Most are still in my head, thank goodness."

"What makes them unique?" Wade asked, his attention directed solely on her. She couldn't look at him now, not when he seemed to bank on her every word. In those western clothes and tan Stetson, he looked very much like the old Wade Beaumont. But she'd been fooled once before, this time she would protect her heart. She kept her focus straight ahead as the sun made a hasty retreat, cooling the warm evening air.

"My designs were all made with gemstones. A piece of jade or turquoise held the garment together in distinct ways, either at the front or the back, sometimes on the straps. In the beginning, I worked up several pieces, sewing them by hand and adding whatever stones I had or could buy inexpensively. But I wanted higher-quality gems like amber and topaz. I learned a lot about stones, hoping to work with a larger variety one day.

"Because the gems were all different colors and all of different quality, each piece of clothing was one-of-a-kind. I sold a few to high-end boutiques and soon I was getting requests. But the gems were costly and I began formulating a plan to start my own company."

"GiGi Designs, right?"

Gina nodded and she couldn't help but smile. "Everyone thought the name stood for my initials, Gina Grady, but actually, I had designed a logo and the tag that I fastened to the clothes read, Gina's Gems."

Gina glanced at Wade and caught him smiling. "Catchy."

"I think so, too," she said, diverting her gaze from Wade's beautiful smile and tantalizing mouth, while trying to block out the look of admiration on his face.

Rio snorted and Gina laid her hand along his long neck, stroking him absently as they continued walking along.

Wade looked straight ahead. "We're almost there."

There was a cropping of tall mesquite trees bordering the Buckley and Beaumont spreads, a long row of them appeared to be the dividing line. Wade led her to that area, dropping the lead rope from Rio. Apparently the horse knew the terrain. He wandered off only a few feet away. "You should have your company, Gina. Sounds like it was what you were meant to do."

"I will one day. I'm sure of that."

Wade took hold of her hand. "Come here," he said, guiding her to an area just beyond the trees. She viewed a large open crate and peered inside to find a mama border collie with five pups lying by her side on a quilt; two of the small pups were nuzzling on their mother voraciously, the others were fast asleep. "Oh, my. They are so sweet!" She turned to Wade, but his eyes were on the pups. "Is that your Lily?"

Wade shook his head. "No, Lily's gone now. Sugar is her daughter and now she's got pups of her own. I brought them out here for some peace and quiet today. I think Sugar likes it here. I'll bring them back to the barn later tonight."

Lily had been Wade's dog growing up. She'd been so gentle and sweet and a great herder. Wade had loved her.

She watched him bend to pet Sugar and the mama

looked up at him with adoring eyes. "That's a good girl," Wade said, stroking her coat lovingly. "You're a good mama, aren't you?"

Gina bent, too, and together they watched the little pups. "How old are they?"

"My uncle said she gave birth three weeks ago."

Gina watched the black-and-white little bundles as they woke, one right after the other, some scrambling for a spot by their mother, ready to suckle, others climbing over each other in the crate. One looked scrawnier than the rest and, instead of the common black-and-white coloring, had a coat of red and brown and white. Gina couldn't help picking that one up.

"Is that the one you like?"

Gina nodded. "I'm a sucker for the underdog."

Wade looked into her eyes for a moment then patted the little pup's head. "I'm thinking of taking one."

Surprised, Gina kept her expression even, hugging the pup a little tighter. "Really? I wouldn't think you'd have time for a dog."

"I'd make time. I'm ready for a commitment. So, you like this one the best?"

"They're all adorable, Wade. The choice is yours. Doesn't matter which one I'd pick."

Wade cocked her half a smile. "Oh, but it does matter."

I'm ready for a commitment.

An unexpected thrill coursed through her body and Gina shoved aside the heartwarming thoughts that accompanied that feeling. She wouldn't let her mind wander down that path.

She reminded herself of Wade's ruthless, calculating behavior towards her. She didn't trust him.

Puppies or not, Gina couldn't fall victim to him again. She put the tiny puppy back into the crate. Immediately, he nudged aside one of his siblings, to get to the mother. "He's a fighter."

"You're a good judge of character," Wade said, watching her with those intent penetrating eyes.

"Am I? Seems to me I messed up a few times in my life."

Wade nodded, a serious expression crossing his features. He spoke softly. "I've done the same, Gina. But I plan to remedy that."

Gina closed her eyes briefly, blocking out the sincere tone in his voice. Then she rose. "I think I'd better get going now."

Wade didn't hesitate. "Let's ride back." With a protest ready on her lips, Wade added quickly, "I promised to get you home in twenty minutes. It's faster this way."

She watched him mount Rio, those long legs lifting up and over the saddle, before he settled himself on and reached down for her hand.

She could either take the long walk back with Wade, with thoughts of commitments and puppies plaguing her every step, or she could be home in a few minutes, the downside being she'd have to share a saddle and the close proximity with him.

"Don't be afraid, Gina," Wade said, leaning down,

coaxing her with those deep-green eyes and an open expression on his face.

But Gina was afraid. She didn't want to lose her grip on the anger and resentment she held. She opted for the fast ride. She took his hand and he lifted her up, placing her in front of him on the saddle.

He wrapped his arms around her waist and handed her the reins. His breath was warm and rousing as he whispered in her ear, "You're in control now, honey."

Gina laced her fingers through the reins, nudged Rio forward, her heart beginning to melt like butter on a hot griddle.

"Glad you realized that, Wade."

His soft caressing chuckle from behind sent shivers.

She felt anything but in control, in truth, she thought she was *losing* all control.

Fast.

Gina spent the next two days with Sarah, working on wedding favors, seating arrangements and going over the plans for the ceremony. She hadn't seen Wade, but heard from both Roy and Mr. Buckley that the men had had their tuxedo fittings and then had gone out for drinks afterward.

Roy wanted no part of a bachelor party, but secretly Gina had joined troops with the two other bridesmaids to throw Sarah a quick bridal-shower luncheon. And Dottie Beaumont had offered up her home.

Gina sat beside Sarah with Kay Buckley and Dottie in the parlor along with several of Sarah's friends from the high school where she was now employed as a college counselor. Both Roy and Sarah had settled for a life in El Paso, working in jobs they loved.

After they'd finished a lunch catered by one of El Paso's finest eateries, cake was served and the gifts were opened.

"Let's see," Gina began, looking at the list she'd marked down, keeping track of which guests gave which gift. "You have three sets of sexy lingerie, apple nectar body oils and lotions, a bottle of French perfume to go along with a full case of French wine generously given to you by principal Carol Donaldson and a half dozen Waterford wine goblets donated by the rest of the staff. I say forget the wedding and skip straight to the honeymoon!"

The ladies laughed and Sarah smiled. "I don't think so. I've been wanting this wedding for a long time, but Roy would surely take you up on it, Gina."

"Sounds good to me," Roy said, coming in the front door, his eyes only on Sarah. "I can't wait to get to the honeymoon part."

Wade came in next, looking handsome in a crisp pair of jeans and a forest-green shirt, the color highlighting the deep hue of his eyes. He searched and found Gina instantly, his gaze focused solely on her face.

Gina's breath caught. Her throat tightened. She didn't like the effect Wade had on her, but she couldn't deny that she'd missed him. Just seeing him now, with all the other single females in the room, gazing at him as if he were a sweet creamy dessert they'd like to devour, put her nerves on edge. Wade, the wealthy, handsome prodigal son, returning to his childhood home, made a great catch for a local girl.

"You boys crashing the party?" Dottie asked, her gaze flowing from Roy to Wade. Gina saw the love and admiration she had for her nephew in that one solitary look. Wade may not have had a mother or a real father, but Lee and Dottie Beaumont had loved him like their own son. He'd been fortunate to have them in his life, *all* of his life. Gina had missed that. She'd missed that unconditional love and the looks of admiration she'd once received from her parents.

Wade glanced her way again and she blinked, uncomfortable with the warmth in his eyes, the softness in his face.

"This is a shower, so I'm here to shower my bride with a gift of my own. Thanks to Wade and his help the past few days, I was able to finish it on time. Come on outside. Your wedding present is waiting."

"Roy, what did you do?" Sarah asked quietly, but with a note of pleasant surprise in her voice.

"Come outside, sweetheart. I can't bring it in."

"Well, for heaven's sake, I'm going outside," Kay Buckley said to the women, "I just love surprises!"

The rest of the women followed.

Gina was the last to rise, making a final note on

her gift list. When she reached the door, Wade was waiting for her.

"Hi," he said, his eyes set on her.

Gina took a swallow and stood rigidly. She spoke with formality, "Hello, Wade."

He chuckled and drew her into his arms, his hands wrapping around her waist, tugging her close. Before she could protest, his lips met hers in a quick, almost chaste, kiss.

Gina backed up and stared at him. "Why did you do that?"

Wade's mouth quirked up quickly. "Couldn't help myself. Haven't seen you in two days."

Another chink in her armor fell away. She pulled in a deep breath. "Wade, you shouldn't…I mean, we can't…I don't think it's—"

He put a halting finger to her lips. "Shh. You think too much. Come on," he said, taking her hand and leading her outside to the front driveway. "You have to see what Roy's done for Sarah."

And as soon as she spotted the car, gift-wrapped with a giant wedding-white bow, memories flooded in of that summer, driving around in Sarah's old, but very classic 1966 Ford Mustang. This car wasn't the original, but Roy had outdone himself renovating a replica of the model.

By far, the cherry-red convertible with tufted leather seats had been Sarah's favorite possession and she'd driven it until the darn car had no more drive left.

"And my thanks go to Wade here," Roy was

telling the bridal-shower ladies, "for donating and flying in the finishing parts, not to mention helping me work on it these past two days to get the renovation done before the wedding."

Those female eyes again shifted to Wade, then moved down to their joined hands, each one of the women giving Gina a look of envy. For once, Gina was glad she hadn't broken the connection. She glanced up at Wade. "You did that for Roy and Sarah?" she asked, her voice elevated. She couldn't conceal her surprise.

Wade gave her a quick nod.

"It was very kind of you."

Wade drew his brows up. "That *almost* sounded like a compliment."

Gina shook her head. "Sorry, but you confuse me."

Wade let go a heavy sigh. "I'm making it my mission in life to unconfuse you."

With that, he leaned in and kissed the side of her head, brushing his lips into her hair.

Which only confused Gina all the more.

"Sarah, don't pair me up with Wade, okay?"

Sarah's soft-blue eyes went wide with surprise. "Why not?" They stood in the church vestibule and were only minutes away from the wedding rehearsal. Gina knew this was asking a lot of her friend.

"Because I don't want to walk down the aisle with him. Can't you send me down with Paul?"

Sarah shook her head. "I'm sorry. You know

Paul's the best man. He's been Roy's good friend forever. And, well, I *had* to ask Joanie to be my matron of honor," Sarah explained. "I was maid of honor in her wedding just last year. It's only right. Otherwise it would have been you, Gina."

"Of course she should be your matron of honor. I know you two have worked together for years at the school and Joanie has been a good friend." Gina didn't want to make the bride feel guilty, yet she suspected something else was going on here. "What about Tim?"

"You mean, break up Tim and Tanya? They'd kill me. Those two are inseparable and their wedding is coming up in six months. Wouldn't want to cause any trouble in paradise."

Gina narrowed her eyes at Sarah. "You're match-making, aren't you?"

Sarah twirled a finger around one long blond strand of hair. A definite sign of guilt, as Gina recalled from their early days at UCLA when Sarah had tried setting her up on blind dates. This time, Sarah didn't try to conceal her plans. She shrugged. "Why not? I have a lot to make up for. If it weren't for me…you and Wade—"

"Wade and I wouldn't have ended up together, Sarah. So, you don't have to feel guilty. Sooner or later, I would have seen him for the kind of man he truly is."

"Oh, you mean, sweet, good-natured, gorgeous and *sexy as sin?*"

Gina's eyes popped open wide. "How would you know that?"

Sarah grinned. "He is, isn't he? God, Gina. The way he looks at you, can't you give him a break?"

Gina let go a deep sigh. "We tried, twice. Both times ended in disaster. And don't say the third time's the charm. That's just a cliché and it's not true."

Sarah lowered her lashes and shook her head. "Sorry, but I disagree. And there's nothing I can do about the wedding party. It's all set. You and Wade are a couple, at least for my wedding." But when Sarah looked up, there wasn't regret in her eyes, but sheer, unabashed hope.

Gina peered down the corridor and found Wade with Roy and the other wedding ushers waiting for the minister to begin the rehearsal. He glanced her way and their gazes locked for a long moment. Gina wondered if she was looking into the face of the sweet, caring, honorable man she had once loved. Was Sarah right? Everything inside screamed at her to be careful, to watch her step, to keep her guard up, while the power of those keen green eyes told her to do just the opposite.

When the organist began to play the traditional wedding march, Sarah's excitement bubbled over. "Here we go," she said, taking Gina's hand. "I'm so happy right now, I can barely stand it. I want the same for you, Gina. Every girl should get the man of her dreams." With that, Wade approached taking long confident strides. "Looks like yours is coming for you now."

Gina closed her eyes briefly, wishing she didn't feel

exactly the same way. Only she wasn't bubbling over with joy like Sarah at the thought. No, she gazed at the handsome, appealing man standing before her now with trepidation, wondering about her unknown future.

"Are you ready to walk down the aisle with me, honey?"

It was a loaded question and one to which Gina could only grunt an unintelligible reply.

Wade laced her arm through his, an unmistakable twinkle in his eyes and a rare but striking smile on his face.

Gina turned to face the long narrow aisle leading to the altar. She imagined what it would be like tomorrow in the tiny romantic chapel in the canyon with family and friends filling the pews, bouquets of pink lilies with streaming large white satin bows lining each aisle, the minister welcoming the wedding guests and Sarah speaking vows of love and devotion.

Sarah and Roy had had a bumpy journey to the altar, but they'd found their way. Gina didn't think it was possible for her and Wade.

Before they took their first steps down the aisle, Wade leaned over, whispering in her ear, "Trust me, baby. We'll be good together."

The warmth and power of those words seeped into her, knocking loose even more chinks in her quickly crumbling armor. But Gina was a survivor, someone who had learned how to protect herself through the most difficult of times. She wouldn't make it easy for him. After the wedding, Gina didn't doubt that they would go their separate ways. "Trust you, Wade? If only I could."

But instead of putting him off, her statement only brought his lips up in another deep and stunning smile.

Twelve

"Wade, let me straighten that tie," Aunt Dottie said, standing close behind and catching his reflection from the bedroom mirror. She'd kept the room he had shared with Sam pretty much intact, complete with baseball trophies, school pennants and family pictures on the wall. Wade was glad she hadn't changed anything. He'd always thought of this place as home, even after he'd moved to Houston with his father and later relocated out west to California.

When she was through with the tie, she faced him and patted his shoulders like she had when he was a small boy. "You're a handsome devil, Wade Beaumont, all grown up now, running your own business." Her eyes were soft on him. "In that tuxedo, you'll turn every female head."

"Thanks for the help. And I only want to turn one female head today."

"That little gal giving you trouble?" Uncle Lee asked, stepping into the bedroom, looking as uncomfortable as a man could get wearing a three-piece suit.

Wade faced the mirror to run a comb through his hair. "She's stubborn."

Aunt Dottie said, "I like to say she's strong in character."

"Hardheaded," Wade rebutted, setting down the comb.

"A woman who knows her own mind," Aunt Dottie reasoned.

Wade nearly snorted, "Driving me out of mine."

"But worth every minute of it." Aunt Dottie tipped her chin for all the independent women in the world.

"I wouldn't be going through this if she wasn't."

Uncle Lee sighed, coming to stand beside him. "You know I felt the same way about your aunt a few decades ago. I had to wear her down."

"Hmph." His aunt smoothed out the wrinkles in her soft floral dress.

"Charmed her." His uncle's eyes lit with amusement.

"And tell Wade what you did when that didn't work," she said, fussing with her updo.

"I swept her off her feet," he said, with a decided puff of the chest.

Aunt Dottie walked over to lace her arm through her husband's. She looked at him lovingly. "More like you kidnapped me, Lee. Drove me over the state line and—"

"You went willingly, Dot, as I recall."

Wade had heard this story countless times in the past, but he didn't mind hearing it once more. Seeds of inspiration were beginning to grow in his mind. Wade wasn't going to let Gina get away this time.

"I did go willingly, Lee. Haven't regretted it a day in my life."

Lee squeezed her hand, then brought his gaze up to look into Wade's eyes. "Son, if you've got your sights set on a strong-minded woman, then you've got to outthink her."

"It's in the works, Uncle Lee."

Wade grabbed his wallet and the keys to his rental car, one he'd picked solely for tonight. "You look pretty Aunt Dottie." He kissed her cheek and smiled. "I'll see you both at the wedding."

"You're sure you don't want to drive with us into town?" his uncle asked.

Wade grinned. "I need my own car if I'm going to do any kidnapping tonight."

With that, Wade left the two of them standing there speechless, their mouths ready to fall open.

"Sarah looks breathtaking," Gina said, watching her friend greet the wedding guests at the reception in the Canyon Ballroom, a lovely intimate room adjacent to the church. She'd managed to get through the ceremony with Wade by her side every second, before, during and afterward. The only time they separated was at the altar, when the ladies stood up for the bride and the men positioned themselves next to a very eager groom.

Wade wrapped his arm around Gina's waist and leaned in close. "*You* look breathtaking," he whispered. "You're the most beautiful woman here."

Gina's toes curled. His nearness, his demeanor today, the caressing way his eyes traveled over her body, warmed her in ways she didn't think possible. She cast him a quick glance. Wade had never looked more appealing, wearing that black tuxedo like a second skin, confidant, sure and so handsome that he stole her breath.

The bride and groom had their opening dance, then Sarah danced with her father and Gina couldn't help but envy her. With Gina's future so unsure, she wondered if ever she married, who would walk her down the aisle? Who would take her into his arms lovingly and sweep her away in that father/daughter dance. It was times like these when Gina missed her parents the most.

Wade's uncle Lee came to stand beside her. He wrapped an arm around her waist. "You and Wade make a fine couple," he said, with a wink. "Walking down that aisle together, gave me notions, girl."

Gina had a protest on her lips to say she and Wade were not a couple, but Uncle Lee's eyes shone just too bright, his face was too sincere and Gina found she didn't want to disappoint the man. "Thank you," she said, and when she met Wade's eyes, she found his approval.

They danced once, the obligatory wedding party invited up to share the dance floor with the bride and groom, as pictures were snapped and then they retired to their seats for dinner.

The round table seated the entire wedding party and when the meal was through, Wade took Gina's hand, placing it on his thigh. Every time he smiled at her with those green eyes, Gina felt herself losing her grip.

"I won't be coming back to work at Triple B, Wade," she began. "Even though you said I still have a job there, it's not what I want."

"I know and I agree."

That surprised her. "You do?"

He nodded, his eyes still soft on her. She'd thought her announcement might have angered him. "You should pursue your own dreams. You should start your own company."

Gina felt somewhat validated. "Thank you for that."

"For what? Realizing that you're a capable woman with a lot to offer. That you have talent and drive and that you deserve a chance, a real chance at doing what you love to do."

Gina smiled, unsure of his intentions. "Are you trying to charm me?"

"God I hope so. Is it working?"

Gina chuckled. She'd never seen Wade so forthright, so open. And while it frightened her, she couldn't help but enjoy his company this evening. "I'm not sure how I feel right now."

When the band began a slow country ballad, Wade rose. "Dance with me?" he asked, offering up his hand.

Gina thought better of it, she knew she wasn't immune to Wade, but as she glanced around the joy-filled room, she couldn't help but want to share in the festivities a little. She took a leap of faith and placed her hand in his.

"Why not? I love this song," she said as Wade guided her to the edge of the dance floor.

"And I love any excuse to hold you in my arms," he said, bringing her in close enough to smell his familiar musky scent. He wrapped his arms around her tight and between the musk and intimate proximity, the reminder of that one blissful night they spent in Catalina rushed into her thoughts.

She closed her eyes and absorbed the music, the heat of the night and the thrill of being in Wade's arms again. Wade's lips teased her temples as he kissed her gently there, whispering in her ear. "I've named the pup, GiGi. I want her to be ours."

Gina popped her eyes open. "Ours?"

Wade smiled. "Yours and mine. That's what ours means."

"But how? It isn't possible. We can't—"

Wade put a stopping finger to her lips. "We can. Anything's possible."

Gina opened her mouth to debate the issue, but Wade's lips met hers in a soul-searing kiss that nearly wiped all rational thought from her head. When she finally opened her eyes, completely breathless, she stared up at him.

"Let's get out of here. I want to be alone with you."

"We can't leave," she said through tight lips. "We're in the wedding party."

"We've taken more pictures than they'll ever need and have done everything we were here to do.

"They haven't cut the cake yet."

"They won't miss us, sweetheart. And once they have cake, the guests will start leaving. We've done our part. Come away with me."

Gina resisted benignly, "Where?"

But Wade had already begun tugging her toward the door. "You'll see."

"You've got to be kidding," Gina said, standing beside Wade's rented convertible Porsche in front of a small lake that bordered the Beaumont ranch, holding a white thong swimsuit that looked suspiciously like the one she'd discarded on Catalina island.

They'd taken a wind-blown drive, letting the breeze and soft rock music steal them away. Now, Wade stood by the car, unfastening his tie. "It's hot, honey. I'm going in for a dip."

"And you expect me to go in with you?" Gina's voice elevated to the incredulous level.

Wade came forward and lifted her bottom onto the hood of the expensive silver sports car. He trapped her between his large hands. He leaned forward, his eyes intense, but his voice a simple soft caress. "I love you, Gina. Get used to hearing me say that. I love you. But I know you can't love me back until you truly trust me."

Stunned, Gina couldn't respond.

I love you, Gina.

"I've never said those words to another woman. And I've been trying so damn hard to get you back. I want you in my life. But first—"

"I have to trust you," she said softly, finally finding her voice.

"That's right. I'm hoping this helps," he said, removing something from his tuxedo jacket. He placed it into her hand and closed her palm with his. "This was my mother's. It's all I have left of her and I want you to have it."

Gina opened her hand slowly, then gasped when she saw the brooch, a sea of tiny flawless diamonds and in the center the most perfect gem she'd ever seen. Jade.

"To start up your gem collection for your company."

"I can't take this," she said, genuinely touched. "Really, Wade. This is…this is so sweet, so kind, but I can't." And as she glanced once again at the exquisite stone, she noted, "It's the perfect match to your eyes."

"I have my mother's eyes. My father gave it to her just months before he lost her."

"He must have loved her a lot. Maybe that's why he was so—"

"Shh. I don't want to talk about him. I want you to keep it."

"But it's yours."

"That's right. And you're going to be mine."

With that, Wade smiled and began undressing one bit at a time, leaving a trail of clothes all he way down to the moonlit lake waters. She watched him dive in and come up from the water, his eyes piercing and passionate. "Trust me, Gina."

It was a request.

A plea.

And an invitation she couldn't ignore.

He loved her.

She felt the clarity of that truth, deep down in her heart. She believed him and as astonishing as that seemed, she felt the rightness of it all, finally, simply.

It was that easy.

Gina scrambled out of her clothes and slipped on the thong while Wade was busy underwater. She approached the lake now, meeting her fear, understanding it for what it was and finally being able to overcome the dread that had always plagued her.

Wade came up from the water and stood, half in, half out, a mythical god with the lake dripping from his skin, beckoning her with his eyes and one outstretched hand.

She stepped in and reached him, taking his hand. "I trust you, Wade," she said, knowing in her heart, he would never do anything to misplace that trust again.

Wade kissed her then, his mouth cold from the swim, but she felt his heat reaching out, touching her.

And together, they moved through the water.

* * *

Later, dripping wet and cold, their clothes thrown on haphazardly, they ran hand in hand into the Beaumont barn, their laughter rousing the sleeping pups.

Gina glanced at the precious litter, too happy to worry about their ruined sleep.

Breathless and burning with desire, she stared into Wade's hungry eyes.

"This is where it all began," he said.

Gina glanced at the wool blanket hanging up along a stall and the stack of hay that had once been their bed. She'd given Wade everything that night. "I've never stopped loving you, Wade. You were always there. I couldn't get rid of you, though I tried. You were my first."

Wade took her into his arms. "I plan on being your last. Until the day I die."

Gina nodded, swallowing the lump in her throat. "Okay."

Wade smiled. "Okay?"

Gina smiled back.

"We already have a family. You, me and GiGi. Wonder how she'll like my house on the beach."

"She'll love it," Gina said, peering down at the pup with the unusual colors.

"Will you?" he asked, reaching around to unzip her ruined bridesmaid gown.

"I think so," she said softly, staring into his eyes.

"And will you let me be your partner, in business and in life?"

He slipped the zipper down, notch by notch, then reached up to expose her shoulders. He kissed her there, making her head swim with delicious thoughts.

"I will, but you won't boss me around."

Wade kissed her lips. "You won't let me."

Gina smiled then and wrapped her arms around his neck, tugging him in to mate their mouths. She kissed him soundly, freely, giving him her trust, her love and her heart. "I'm glad we've got that straight."

Wade slipped her dress off, letting it puddle at her feet. She stepped over it, standing fully unclothed before him.

"I wanted you for my wife the minute I laid eyes on you," he said, quietly, reverently, his gaze gently scanning her body.

Gina removed his shirt, unzipped his pants. "You're a fast worker, sweetheart. Only took you nine years."

They stood naked before one another.

Then together they lowered down onto the hay.

They joined their bodies, bonding themselves for the future, in the barn, on a soft patch of straw, where they'd first found each other.

"Some things are just worth the wait."

* * * * *

THE ROYAL HOUSE OF NIROLI
Always passionate, always proud

The richest royal family in the world—united
by blood and passion,
torn apart by deceit and desire

Nestled in the azure blue of the Mediterranean Sea,
the majestic island of Niroli has prospered for cen-
turies. The Fierezza men have worn the crown with
passion and pride since ancient times. But now, as
the king's health declines, and his two sons have
been tragically killed, the crown is in jeopardy.

The clock is ticking—a new heir must be found
before the king is forced to abdicate. By royal decree
the internationally scattered members of the Fierezza
family are summoned to claim their destiny. But any
person who takes the throne must do so according
to The Rules of the Royal House of Niroli. Soon
secrets and rivalries emerge as the descendents of
this ancient royal line vie for position and power.
Only a true Fierezza can become ruler—a person
dedicated to their country, their people…and their
eternal love!

FIVE minutes later she was standing immobile in front of the study's window, her original purpose of coming in forgotten, as she stared in shocked horror at the envelope she was holding. Waves of heat followed by icy chill surged through her body. She could hardly see the address now through her blurred vision, but the crest on its left-hand front corner stood out, its *royal* crest, followed by the address: *HRH Prince Marco of Niroli...*

She didn't hear Marco's key in the apartment door, she didn't even hear him calling out her name. Her shock was so great that nothing could penetrate it. It encased her in a kind of bubble, which only concentrated the torment of what she was suffering and

branded it on her brain so that it could never be forgotten. It was only finally pierced by the sudden
opening of the study door as Marco walked in.

"Welcome home, *Your Highness*. I suppose I
ought to curtsy." She waited, praying that he would
laugh and tell her that she had got it all wrong, that
the envelope she was holding, addressing him as
Prince Marco of Niroli, was some silly mistake. But
like a tiny candle flame shivering vulnerably in the
dark, her hope trembled fearfully. And then the look
in Marco's eyes extinguished it as cruelly as a hand
placed callously over a dying person's face to stem
their last breath.

"Give that to me," he demanded, taking the
envelope from her.

"It's too late, Marco," Emily told him brokenly.
"I know the truth now…." She dug her teeth in her
lower lip to try to force back her own pain.

"You had no right to go through my desk," Marco
shot back at her furiously, full of loathing at being
caught off-guard and forced into a position in which
he was in the wrong, making him determined to find
something he could accuse Emily of. "I trusted
you…."

Emily could hardly believe what she was hearing.
"No, you didn't trust me, Marco, and you didn't
trust me because you knew that I couldn't trust you.
And you knew that because you're a liar, and liars
don't trust people because they know that they themselves cannot be trusted." She not only felt sick, she
also felt as though she could hardly breathe. "You

are Prince Marco of Niroli…. How could you not tell me who you are and still live with me as intimately as we have lived together?" she demanded brokenly.

"Stop being so ridiculously dramatic," Marco demanded fiercely. "You are making too much of the situation."

"*Too much?*" Emily almost screamed the words at him. "When were you going to tell me, Marco? Perhaps you just planned to walk away without telling me anything? After all, what do my feelings matter to you?"

"Of course they matter." Marco stopped her sharply. "And it was in part to protect them, and you, that I decided not to inform you when my grandfather first announced that he intended to step down from the throne and hand it on to me."

"To protect me?" Emily nearly choked on her fury. "Hand on the throne? No wonder you told me when you first took me to bed that all you wanted was sex. You *knew* that was the only kind of relationship there could ever be between us! You *knew* that one day you would be Niroli's king. No doubt you are expected to marry a princess. Is she picked out for you already, your *royal* bride?"

* * * * *

HARLEQUIN®

Mediterranean NIGHTS™

*Experience the glamour and elegance of cruising the
high seas with a new 12-book series....*

MEDITERRANEAN NIGHTS

Coming in July 2007...

SCENT OF A WOMAN

by

Joanne Rock

When Danielle Chevalier is invited to an exclusive
conference aboard *Alexandra's Dream,* she knows it
will mean good things for her struggling fragrance
company. But her dreams get a setback when she
meets Adam Burns, a representative from a large
American conglomerate.

Danielle is charmed by the brusque American—
until she finds out he means to compete with her bid
for the opportunity that will save her family business!

n o c t u r n e™

**DON'T MISS THE RIVETING CONCLUSION
TO THE RAINTREE TRILOGY**

RAINTREE: SANCTUARY

by *New York Times* bestselling author

BEVERLY BARTON

Mercy, guardian of the Raintree
homeplace, takes a stand against
the Ansara wizards to battle for
the Clan's future.

*On sale July,
wherever books are sold.*

REQUEST YOUR FREE BOOKS!

2 FREE NOVELS PLUS 2 FREE GIFTS!

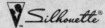

Passionate, Powerful, Provocative!

Silhouette® Desire

COMING NEXT MONTH

#1807 THE CEO'S SCANDALOUS AFFAIR—
Roxanne St. Claire
Dynasties: The Garrisons
He needed her for just one night—but the repercussions of their sensual evening could last a lifetime!

#1808 HIGH-SOCIETY MISTRESS—Katherine Garbera
The Mistresses
He will stop at nothing to take over his business rival's company…including bedding his enemy's daughter and making her his mistress.

#1809 MARRIED TO HIS BUSINESS—Elizabeth Bevarly
Millionaire of the Month
To get his assistant back this CEO plans to woo and seduce her. But he isn't prepared when she ups the stakes on *his* game.

#1810 THE PRINCE'S ULTIMATE DECEPTION—
Emilie Rose
Monte Carlo Affairs
It was a carefree vacation romance. Until she discovers she's having an affair with a prince in disguise.

#1811 ROSSELLINI'S REVENGE AFFAIR—
Yvonne Lindsay
He blamed her for his family's misery and sought revenge in a most passionate way!

#1812 THE BOSS'S DEMAND—Jennifer Lewis
She was pregnant with the boss's baby—but wanted more than just the convenient marriage he was offering.